"I feel a bit like the first time we arrived home after our honeymoon."

Her eyes blurred at the sudden vivid memory. They had both been so young, still teenagers, nervous and excited at the same time. And they had both been so much in love.

"For me to carry you over the threshold this time, you'd have to sit on my lap."

She searched his face for a moment, but there was nothing in his expression now except jubilation and amusement. Her heart lightened.

A relieved laugh escaped her. "That might be safer than hauling me over your shoulder in a fireman's lift, then dumping me on the floor as soon as you took two steps inside."

"Let's see shall we?"

MARY HAWKINS lives in Austrailia with her husband; they have three grown children. Her first inspirational novel, *Search for Tomorrow*, was voted the second most favorite contemporary by **Heartsong Presents** readers.

Books by Mary Hawkins

HEARTSONG PRESENTS
HP42—Search for Tomorrow
HP101—Damaged Dreams
HP129—Search for Yesterday

Search for Today

Mary Hawkins

A sequel to *Search for Yesterday*

Heartsong Presents

To my brother, Stan Pedler,
who has come out of personal trauma and grief
to be an effective witness for Christ
through the "New Light Ministries"
in the Torres Strait islands.

A note from the Author:
I love to hear from my readers! You may write to me at
the following address: **Mary Hawkins**
Author Relations
P.O. Box 719
Uhrichsville, OH 44683

ISBN 1-55748-970-X

SEARCH FOR TODAY

Cover illustration by Kay Salem.

PRINTED IN THE U.S.A.

one

Because God is faithful. . .
  My tomrrows are safe in His hands.
Because I love Him. . .
  My yesterdays He'll work out for good.
But today. . .
  Ah, today. . .
I must walk with Him hand in hand!

❧

Her silky hair was a mass of golden curls beneath a circlet of red baby roses and frivolous tulle. His heart ached as he watched her slow procession down the aisle toward him. She was more beautiful than he had ever seen her. More beautiful even than on that other wonderful day that now seemed so long ago, the day when she had married him.

Serious, deep blue eyes met his for a long moment. Something flickered in their depths. Something he couldn't read.

Then she was past him, continuing her slow progress to the beat of the wedding march, eventually obscured by the standing congregation as she moved to her place next to Will. Art closed his eyes, swallowing the painful lump in his throat. He clenched his fist on the arm-rest of his wheel-chair and felt like pounding something. . .anything. . . .

Beth was his wife. *His wife!* And despite his useless legs he still loved her. Loved her desperately. What had happened to them? When had it all gone so wrong? Why didn't she—?

"Isn't Mummy beautiful!"

He glanced sideways at the small miniature of Beth

standing beside him. Jacqueline's wide eyes met his. The admiration and pride in them changed abruptly. The sudden trace of wariness on the dainty little face cut into him.

"Your mother is always beautiful, Jacky."

He forced himself to smile, but his harsh whisper did not change her expression, and she quickly looked away. Robbie peered around her, his eyes wide. Art smiled at him too, and his small son's shy grin pulled at his heart. At least Robbie seemed to have accepted his father's return into their lives much better than Jacky had.

He should never have walked out on them all those months ago. At the time, it had been the only way he had been able to handle the increasing tension, the arguments, the fear. Now he recognized just how much of a coward he had been.

That last bitter row between Beth and himself had really scared him. He had lost control. Had even lashed out at her! Her flushed face and angry accusations had spat fury right back at him.

That's when the realization had hit him, with overwhelming bitterness as never before: he was a wretched sinner. Certainly at least one frustrated, angry schoolteacher had tried to tell him. Certainly his own very religious parents had tried to drum it into him often enough. All of them were right. He was just no good. He should never have married Beth Stevens.

So he had packed up. Gone.

There was a stir behind him, a few murmurs of admiration. Art swung his head toward the church entrance. For a moment he stared. A mist of pride filmed his eyes, and his own pain receded a little. The bride was radiant.

At least this was one thing he had done right, even if the end result for himself had been this wheelchair. If it had not been for him, she would not be here today. Gail Brandon would have been killed in the accident that had wiped out her family. She would never have come to the Darling Downs. But then, if he had not been driving that semi-trailer at that particular place, at that particular moment. . . ? As he always did, Art pushed the ghastly memories away.

Gail had paused. Her eyes were fixed steadily toward the front of the church. The light in them made him swallow rapidly. And then the tall figure of his brother-in-law and best friend, Jim Stevens, moved past him to join her. She slipped her hand in his elbow. The organ music swelled to a crescendo and together they started down the aisle.

As they reached Art, Gail gave him a special, warm smile. He grinned up at her, and his smile lingered as they moved slowly past him to at last reach their attendants and the waiting Reverend Rance Telford. For a moment he regretted refusing her request to "give her away" in place of her father.

"There's no way I'd do that from a wheelchair," he'd snarled back at her.

She had scowled right back at him and muttered something about "I don't have anyone else I care enough about."

For a moment he had almost weakened, but he knew just how much he was suffering from the "wheelchair stigma." He wasn't sure whom he disliked the most, people who gave him pitying looks, people who just stared curiously, people who looked briefly and then away, embarrassed, not sure how to talk to a paraplegic in a wheelchair, or people who wanted to know too many details. And there had been some of each when he had arrived at the church. No, he didn't regret his refusal to be part of the wedding party.

Besides, already he was feeling very weary and his back was aching badly. Coming to the wedding had been more of an effort than he had thought it would be. This was his third day of leave from the rehabilitation unit, the second morning without the torturous, daily exercises with the hospital physiotherapists, and his longest time out of the hospital in twelve months.

Beth had been wonderful. His lips curved into a smile. She had certainly helped him as much as she could to recover from the two-hour car trip from Brisbane. It had been his longest since the accident, but he still had not expected the amount of stiffness and pain it had caused.

After the last eighteen months of turmoil and heartbreak, he had been so glad to be back at the Stevens' farm. Feeling part of the family again was wonderful. And yet. . .Art hunched his shoulders.

Even harder than the physical effort of getting into his old, but barely worn suit and tie, getting in and out of the car, the ride to this small church set amidst the grain and cotton farming community of the Darling Downs, had been the memories. Memories that were proving to be strong and heartrending.

With an effort, he forced his mind back to the wedding. Back from memories when he'd been able to walk. When he'd been to his own wedding here, to other special services held in this little building.

Of course, he thought crossly, *this small country church would only have steps and no ramp.* It had been humiliating as well as scary being fussed around as his chair had been lifted and manoeuvered up the steps. Then pews and chairs had been moved around so his chair would fit at the end of a row without being obstructive. But he still felt horribly conspicuous, out of place. . . .

As the wedding ceremony ebbed and flowed around him, Art's weariness increased. He could not sing Gail and Jim's choice of hymn, though not because he did not know it. Once he'd known a lot of hymns much too well, for he had felt his father's belt later if he had not sung them. Those days were long gone, but no way he could sing "To God be the glory, great things He has done," when there was precious little God had ever done for him.

But, he had to admit, he saw something almost awesome about the radiance of the bride and groom as they exchanged vows and rings, as they listened to the Bible reading about love being the most important thing. He watched them bow their heads reverently in prayer.

And Art wondered, not for the first time, how Gail could have recovered as well as she had from the deaths of her fiance and whole family when their car had plunged into his truck. She was by no means a shallow person. In fact, the more he got to know her, the more he admired her. Apparently she had suffered nightmares for months after the accident, and she had had periods of depression.

Never as bad as his though. That first time she had visited him in the hospital. . .He shuddered at the horrible memory of what he had been contemplating, planning. . . what she had by her very visit prevented. . . .

A ripple of laughter swept through the congregation. Art realized that Jim had been given permission to kiss his bride and was doing so very enthusiastically.

"Yuk!"

There was another, louder chorus of laughter. Mrs. Stevens hushed Robbie, and he subsided back on his seat. He looked across and caught his father's eye apprehensively. Art grinned widely at him and winked. A relieved, smile answered him.

Art looked back at the now flushed, even more radiant bridal couple, and then, inevitably, his eyes swung toward the matron of honor. She was looking at him, a smile tilting her beautiful lips. He smiled back, but as she turned her attention away to the continuing service, sharp pain slashed through him.

How long since he and Beth had kissed like that?

He continued to stare at the beautiful woman in the shimmering aqua gown standing beside Gail. He saw her smiling gently across at Will, her tall teenage brother. He watched as she followed Gail and Jim into a back room to sign the marriage's legal papers, and even her straight shoulders and the gleaming back of her head sent a stab of pain through his heart. Jacky was so right. Beth was beautiful.

But her pretty face had not been what had first attracted him to her. There had been plenty of pretty faces only too keen to be seen with the high school football star. Beth had been different. She had a sweetness and innocence about her that had drawn him to her like a magnet. It still did.

"How are you doing, Arthur? Arthur!"

The low insistent voice penetrated through the host of memories of two teenagers not prepared to wait, wanting to take on the world so they could be together for ever. He blinked and stared blindly for a moment at the concerned face of Jean Drew, his mother-in-law's friend and the nursing sister who worked in the Sydney hospital where he had been a patient for far too many months before his transfer to Brisbane. She was studying him professionally, her expression guarded.

At last his mouth twisted in an attempt at a smile. "Fine. Just fine," he muttered hoarsely.

Even as he spoke, he knew it was a stupid lie. He had been sitting too long. His back was more than just aching. The pins and needles had been steadily getting worse, and now he was conscious of the fact that his head was starting to throb abominably. At least it should all be over soon. Surely they would not take too long to sign the register and all the other certificates.

"You don't look it," Jean murmured.

He glared at her for a moment, then his shoulders slumped. "Well, what do you think?"

"I think you should let me organize a lift home for you as soon as possible."

The thought of being able to get away from all the curious eyes, of being able to lie down and ease the pressure on his back, sounded like sheer bliss. The doctor had warned him the trip and wedding could be a bit too adventurous at this stage.

He glanced cautiously toward Jacky and felt relieved that she was turned away, whispering to her brother.

"Beth will worry."

Jean shook her head at him. "Not as much as she will if she has to watch your white face during the reception! Got a headache?"

He snorted loudly. Some people across the aisle turned and stared at him. A soloist had not long finished singing about this being "the day the Lord has made." Now soft music was playing against the background of the murmur of voices which had risen while they waited for the bridal party.

Art glared back at some neighbors and friends of the Stevenses and they looked quickly away. For a brief moment he felt a heel. Then he mentally shrugged. Everyone was feeling so sorry for the poor paralyzed bloke in the wheelchair that he did not think he could take much more. "After they leave the church," he muttered at last.

Relief lightened Jean's expression. She nodded abruptly. Leaving now would mean bed instead of the celebrations at the wedding reception. And he'd had enough of being on a bed the last twelve months. Depression rolled over him in waves. He had always enjoyed parties, and he had been so looking forward to this special day for his old friend Jim and the girl he loved.

When they eventually proceeded down the aisle, Jim and Gail paused beside him. Somehow, he summoned up a smile for them. Jim's handshake was firm and Gail's kiss a little teary. They moved on.

Then Beth was there. Once again Art could not decipher something in his wife's expression. She came closer. Stopped. His heart clenched.

She bent toward him and her delicate perfume invaded his senses. Her lips touched his. For a moment those deep blue eyes stared intently at him, and then she was gone on Will's arm. Art felt as though a flame had briefly touched his mouth.

He sat very still. He only stirred when Marian Stevens leaned over and touched him, gesturing to let her past with her grandchildren. He nodded grimly in response to his mother-in-law's sympathetic smile and moved his chair back slightly. Robbie and Jacky pushed past him excitedly. Then the people filed out after the bridal party, and he carefully avoided the curious eyes once again, only looking around him blindly when the building was almost empty.

His head was feeling more and more as though it would burst, and when Jean at last reappeared and grasped his chair, he could only feel utter relief.

As Jean turned him toward a side door, she said briskly, "I've lined up a couple of guys to help us. That young school-teacher is getting his car."

"Did you tell Beth. . . ?" Then he stopped. There was a rustle of silk and she was there.

"Oh, Art! Are you all right? I thought you looked tired."

"A bit of a headache. Don't fuss."

As soon as the words had exploded from him he was sorry. Her sharp withdrawal from him was more than physical, and quickly he tried to make amends. He managed a weak smile. "Guess the doc was smarter than me after all. Just as well you and Gail organized that Tony bloke to help out in case this happened. Tell the bride and groom I'm sorry. Don't you worry either. All I need is a bed to crash on for a while."

But she was already worried. He knew how valiantly she tried to disguise it from him, but it was there in her clenched fists, the strained smile, the way her eyes avoided his, the way she helped swing his legs so gently into the car.

And he wondered for the thousandth time how long he could bear to have her so burdened by him.

"Please, Beth, enjoy the evening. I'm going to be fine with Tony. At least I've seen Gail and Jim do the deed."

She didn't kiss him again, and he knew she probably wouldn't enjoy the evening.

Beth had been the best thing that had ever happened to him, but how many of her days and evenings had he wrecked forever? And how could he convince her she was only ruining the rest of her life by being tied to a coward of a man with useless legs?

two

Beth shivered in the cool night air and pulled her shawl tighter around her shoulders. She glanced over her shoulder into the backseat of the car. Her gaze lingered on her two children snuggled up each side of Will.

"Still asleep?"

Beth looked across at her mother and nodded. "Out like a light. Will is too." She was silent for a moment, watching the headlights cut through the blackness of the flat countryside. "They should have been in bed hours ago," she said at last.

"One late night won't hurt them," Mrs. Stevens said firmly, grasping the steering wheel tightly. After a moment she added softly, "I'm glad they were already asleep when Bob. . ." Her voice faltered.

Beth felt the tears whelm up again. "I still can't believe it," she said in a choked voice. "One moment Uncle Bob was. . .was wishing Jim and Gail all the best, and. . .and by the time their car had driven off he was gone! Poor Hilda."

Mrs. Stevens was silent. Then she said very softly, "I'm glad Jean was there. It would have been so much harder for Hilda if he'd had the heart attack at home when she was by herself. At least she will know that everything was done for her father that could be."

"I don't think she knows anything at the moment," Beth muttered.

They had all been stunned by the collapse of Bob Garrett. Jim and Gail's car with its clanging tin cans and streamers had barely disappeared before the word had swept through the wedding guests that Bob Garrett had suffered a heart attack, and Jean Drew and the minister, Rance Telford, were giving him CPR. With the help of other guests, they had kept it up until the ambulance had arrived. But it had all been to no avail.

After the ambulance had departed with her father's lifeless body, Hilda Garrett had been in deep shock. She moved like a sleep walker as Jean Drew had at last helped her out to the car to take her home.

"Jean's going to stay with her for a few days," Mrs. Stevens said in a choked voice.

"Oh, Mum," Beth burst out, "life's not fair! As though there hasn't been enough grief and pain. First Hilda's mum died, then my dad, then Art's nearly killed. I don't know how Gail copes so well with her family wiped out like that. There's been all those months with me in Sydney with Art. I thought life might be easier for us all with Art well enough to be moved to Brisbane for further rehabilitation. But now. . .now. . ." Her voice choked as the tears slid down her face.

"Now we keep on trusting the Lord to watch over us and work things out for good as He always has," Mrs. Stevens said in a husky voice.

"Do we?" Beth's voice hardened. "I'm not so sure anymore about. . .about anything."

As soon as the words had burst out of her she regretted them; she even knew they weren't really true. Not anymore. She knew how much her own loss of faith over the last few years had hurt and upset her mother. But since Art had disappeared and then ended up in the hospital, she had been coming to grips more and more with spiritual matters. Her faith was gradually being renewed—but still, at times it was all so hard.

"If God was not looking after us, strengthening us, I don't think I would have coped at all since your father was diagnosed with cancer, Beth. Especially after he died." Mrs. Stevens voice was sad, but filled with conviction. "As for Gail, since she accepted Christ into her life and committed herself to Him, her whole outlook on life has been transformed. You saw for yourself today just how at peace she is, and how happy."

A pang shot through Beth. If only Art. . . .

She had not spent a lot of time with Gail, but from what everyone had told her, Gail was certainly different now. Finding out that God loved her, and responding to His love personally, had transformed the traumatized woman who had gone to help look after Jacky and Robbie last year while Beth had been at the Sydney hospital with Art.

Beth closed her eyes. Once she had thought her own faith in a loving, caring heavenly Father was unshakable. She had been such a keen Christian, but when she had first met Arthur Canley-Smith she been knocked clean off her conservative, narrow pins by his blond good looks, twinkling hazel eyes, and muscular, rugby-type physique.

She had been so sure God would make Art become a Christian. She had prayed so hard, so many times. She had talked to him often about becoming a Christian. After all, she had loved the tall, rugged young teenager so much, anything else had been unthinkable. But God had never seemed to hear her prayer. Now it all seemed such a long time ago.

She remembered something else her mother had once said to her, and shame filled her again. "You were right, Mum," she said abruptly.

Her mother glanced at her but didn't speak. That was something Beth had always loved about her. She always waited, never rushed in with words, waited until you needed her to speak. If only Beth had tried harder herself to follow that example with Art over the years!

"You told me once, years ago, that we sometimes make it very hard for God to answer our prayers when we disobey His warnings and principles." Beth continued sadly, "Like I did when I married an unbeliever."

Her mother didn't speak for a look moment. Then she said softly, "You've changed a lot since Art left you, Beth, and we're still praying for you both."

"Thanks, Mum. We certainly need every prayer available!"

Neither woman spoke again as they completed the drive home. Will woke up as the car moved slowly over the rough track from the main road into the farmhouse.

Beth turned and smiled at him as he yawned loudly. "Almost home, little brother."

"Hey, Sis! Not so much of the *little*," he protested in his uneven tones. "After all, I was big enough to be Jim's best man today. And your escort."

"Oh, so you were," Beth mocked gently. "But you didn't hang around the matron of honor very much, I noticed."

"You both looked after Jim and Gail very well."

There was pride in their mother's voice, and the two smiled at each other behind her back.

Will yawned again as the car crawled to a stop. "Looks like Art's not asleep yet."

Beth felt the tension start to build up in her as she noticed the bedroom light. "He has trouble sleeping when he gets overtired," she said quietly. *And when his muscles spasm, and when his back aches*, she could have added but didn't.

Several minutes later, compassion swamped her as she studied Art's ravaged face as he looked up at her. His hazel eyes were filled with pain and set deep in his pale face.

"Where's Tony?" she asked, hearing the sharp tone in her voice and regretting it immediately as Art's expression tightened.

"I sent him home," he said abruptly. "I appreciated the fact that he had been recruited to bring me home from the church, help me into bed, and baby-sit me. But—he might be the kid's schoolteacher, but he doesn't have much idea of how to make conversation with a stranger, especially someone in a wheelchair. Besides, I thought you'd be home ages ago."

Beth took a deep breath. "So did I. Unfortunately. . .unfortunately. . ." She couldn't continue. Her voice wobbled, and helpless tears started to run down her cheeks.

"Beth?" Art raised himself painfully on one elbow. "What's wrong? What's happened?"

"Uncle. . .Uncle Bob Garrett had a heart attack."

Art reached up to her. She caught his hand and he pulled her down onto the side of the bed. "Is he okay?"

She shook her head. He gave a sharp exclamation. Briefly she told him what had happened. She felt his arms wrap around her, hug her closer. Then somehow she couldn't stop crying. And she knew her tears were not only for the dear old next door neighbor who had been an honorary uncle all her life.

She had not cried wrapped in the security of this man's loving arms for a long, long time. When her sobs at last died away, she realized she was lying on the bed with Art holding her tightly, her head cradled against his shoulder.

She didn't move for some time. Even if she was only lying on top of his blankets, it was sheer bliss being this close to him after such a long time. Then she felt one of Art's legs spasm and jerk. She started to move, but his arms tightened for a moment before he slowly released her.

"I'm sorry, Beth," he whispered.

As she sat up, she looked at him silently, scrubbing at her wet cheeks. What did he mean? Sorry for what?

He answered the query in her face with a grimace. "I'm sorry I can't get you a handkerchief this time."

She stared at him. And then she remembered. The night her father had died, Art had held her. They had not even been officially engaged then. The second time she had cried buckets was the day their daughter was born, and it had suddenly hit her that her father would never see his first grandchild.

Each time, Art had silently let her weep, offering her the shelter of his arms and his love. And then very, very gently and quietly he would reach for a clean handkerchief and mop up her tears.

"We were so close then, Art," she whispered wistfully as they stared at each other. "What happened to us?"

His face went still. Then he turned his face away and she could only see the tension in his jaw. "Life happened to us. Dirty, rotten, stinking life."

She caught her breath on a stab of pain.

Art closed his eyes. "We should never have married, Beth," he added wearily. "We were too young. Our whole outlook on life was. . .is. . .just too, too different. Our backgrounds were too different. You came from a loving family, and mine. . .well, you caught only a brief glimpse once of what mine was like. I was even glad then that my parents had kicked me out before we met."

Beth froze. What was he saying? That there was no hope for their marriage? Eighteen months ago when he had walked out after that last, dreadful row, she had refused to believe it. Certainly after more than six months of silence from him she had almost lost heart and given up. Then she had found out about the accident. She thought the last few months had drawn them close enough to have a good chance to sort things out. . .to start again. But now?

"We have to talk about that last night, Beth."

Fear swamped her. She stood up. "No," she said fiercely, "not now. Not tonight. We're both exhausted." The tears were ready to spill over again, but she hung onto her self-control grimly. "When you aren't so tired, and—"

Art suddenly exploded. "When I'm not tired! When I'm not in the hospital! When the children aren't around. When I'm not what? There's never been a right time since you walked into my hospital room. When, Beth? Nothing's been resolved between us, and I can't stand it anymore!"

Did that mean. . . ? Beth stared at him in horror.

"When I'm not exhausted. When things are more settled," she flared back, "when you're finally discharged from the hospital. When. . .when you. . ." She faltered, and stopped.

Art looked at her steadily. "When I walk again? That's not going to happen, Beth, and it's about time you accepted that fact of life."

"But the doctors said—"

He snorted angrily. "They've said a lot of things that just have not happened. And they did say in the very beginning there was only the slightest chance I might one day be able to move on my feet with walking aids. But it's twelve months now. And they are warning me that's more and more un-likely."

"No," Beth denied sharply, "we've got to believe. There's always hope, and. . .and I've been praying awful hard. And so have a lot of other people."

"Don't start all that religious garbage again," Art started to say furiously, then broke off as the door opened.

His mother-in-law strode into the room. She put her hands on her hips and glared at them both. "Don't you think we've had enough drama for one day? We can hear you all over the house."

They both stared at her blankly.

"Is there anything we can get for you, Art?" Mrs. Stevens asked when neither spoke.

After a moment Art shook his head and looked away.

"Then let Beth get to bed." She added abruptly, "If she goes now, she might be able to get up in time to go to church tomorrow. After all, it will be Easter Sunday." She turned and strode out of the room.

Husband and wife stared at each other in silence. Then Art slowly and carefully pushed himself over onto his side facing away from Beth. Without a word, she pulled back the bedclothes and positioned his legs for him.

"Thank you," he said stiffly.

For a moment, she hesitated, and then touched his shoulder fleetingly. "I. . .I wasn't planning on going to church in the morning without you, Art."

He didn't answer, and after a moment, she sighed and left the room.

❧

The barking of a dog woke Beth the next morning. She had not slept very well, and she reluctantly opened her eyes to look toward the window where the early morning light cast patterns through the lace curtains. As she turned and surveyed her old room, running footsteps sped past in the hallway outside. Robbie was racing outside to play with Bonnie, the young collie dog Hilda Garrett had given the children.

She tensed, waiting for the familiar bang of the old screen door. When it did not come, she relaxed, remembering that was one of the changes Gail had made here during the last few weeks. A new screen door with a proper spring closing device had replaced the old one that had banged almost as long as Beth could remember.

She looked around her old room. Nothing had been changed in here. It had always been her room. When she had boarded in Dalby so she could go to high school, it had still been her room. Even since her marriage at the end of her final year of school, it had always been here when she had gone home for a visit.

Now things would be different. This house was Gail's home now. Inevitably she would want to change things around. Already, new bedroom furniture had been put in the master bedroom for the newlyweds, although at Gail's insistence, Will and Mrs. Stevens still had their usual rooms. The plan was to fix up the old play area on the enclosed veranda for Beth and her family when they visited. And that had been where Art had insisted on sleeping. By himself.

"If I need anything during the night, I'll yell out for Jim or Jean," he had insisted belligerently when they had arrived Thursday, just in time for Beth to rush off to the wedding rehearsal. "It'll give Beth a break," he'd added swiftly.

But she knew that was just an excuse. Beth had been careful not to show how hurt she had felt at his rejection of her help once again. He had been allowed home from the rehabilitation hospital in Brisbane for a few weekend leaves, and she had coped reasonably well from the Saturday morning to the Sunday afternoon. But this Easter weekend would be his longest spell out of the hospital since the accident.

Beth raised her head quickly. Had that been something falling?

There was another distant crash, and she was out of bed like a flash and tearing down the hallway. She heard Art's voice, swearing furiously.

When she raced into the room he was sprawled on the floor beside the bed, trying to raise himself up on his elbows. The bedside table was on its side, the paraphernalia on top of it scattered across the floor.

She gave a frightened gasp and rushed forward to crouch beside him. "Art, whatever were you trying to do?"

He glared at her, threw off her hand on his arm, and swore again. She winced but glared right back.

"What does it look like?" he snarled at her.

After months of rebuffs, his sarcasm was suddenly the last straw. Before she could prevent herself, she snarled right back at him, "It looks like you're being a fool trying to get out of bed by yourself!"

A spark of something like surprise lit his eyes for a moment. A faint gleam of satisfaction filled Beth. Perhaps she had been trying too hard to be nice and obliging these last few months.

Art looked away quickly. With a supreme effort he curled over and lifting one leg at a time positioned them. Then he started trying to push himself into a sitting position. It took considerable restraint for Beth to stand back and watch without lifting a hand to help.

With his eyes averted, he growled harshly at last, "I'm not that big a fool. I was only sitting on the side of the bed. Give me a heave."

_No_ please, _of course,_ Beth thought crossly, but she managed not to say it out loud.

Art succeeded in pushing himself to a sitting position with her help and then glared at her again. There was a movement behind Beth, and an expression of relief crossed his face as he stared past her.

"What's going on?" Will's sleepy voice asked.

"I fell off the side of the bed," Art said crossly in a low voice. He gestured with his head toward the wheelchair at the foot of the low bed. "Bring that over behind me."

Beth did so without speaking. Will looked from one to the other and then said quietly, "If we hold you under each arm and haul you up, we should be able to slip it under you."

"Pull that bedside cabinet over in front of me first," Art said curtly. "I can lean on it and take some of my own weight."

He gave them a few more terse instructions, and before long he was in the wheelchair. Will helped Beth pick up the scattered things from the cabinet and then disappeared with a mumbled excuse.

"I knocked the book off the bed when I turned over. When I sat up and tried to reach down for it I lost my balance," Art muttered at last when Beth did not move.

"Did you hurt yourself anywhere?" Beth asked abruptly.

"I don't think so, but perhaps you'd better check my leg. I think I might have bashed it against the cabinet when I fell."

With stiff fingers Beth started to roll up his pajama leg, then caught her breath at a smear of blood. She let out a sigh of relief when she found the source, a fairly small skin tear.

"Nothing some iodine and a couple of plaster strips won't fix," she said cheerfully.

"If only the rest of me was that easy to fix."

Beth looked up at him swiftly. He was staring down at his legs, and when he raised his eyes to look at her they were full of despair and pain.

"I've got blood trickling down my leg where I bashed myself, and I can't even feel it," he whispered harshly.

Pity flooded through Beth, but she bent her head and

started wiping away the blood. "Well, that's something to be thankful for, isn't it?" He had shown her many times in the last months how he hated being pitied, so she refused to show him any pity now. "I'll just go and raid Mum's first-aid box."

Still not looking at him, she made for the doorway, but his voice stopped her.

"Do you think she'd be very upset if we went straight home after breakfast?"

Beth swung around. Art was staring down at his leg. He looked up at her and the misery in his face made her say without hesitation, "I'm sure she won't. In fact, it doesn't matter if she does."

Not until she was in the kitchen with the box of plaster strips in her hands did she think about how Jacky and Robbie would take their early return home. "Too bad," she muttered to herself grimly, "It's their father's turn to be put first now."

As she strode purposefully back to Art, she suddenly realized how few times until he had been injured had she really put his welfare before that of the children's, or her own, for that matter. Perhaps that was why he had been surprised at her determination to stay in Sydney and let Jim and her mother look after the children for those long months.

As she sat on the bed to attend to the cut, she was very thoughtful. "Art, how about leaving the kids here with Mum? It wouldn't hurt them to miss a few days school."

"No!"

Surprised at his vehement refusal, she looked swiftly at him. She had really thought he would prefer the peace of the empty house for the rest of the Easter weekend, until his leave from the rehabilitation hospital was finished

Monday evening.

"Your mother's going to be busy going to Bob Garret's funeral and knowing her, helping Hilda. I'm real sorry you'll have to miss it. Besides, the kids have been unsettled enough. I've also missed too much of their growing-up days already." His voice was gruff, and he avoided her eyes. "The kids hardly know me as it is. And Robbie told me this morning that Bonnie is really his and Jacky's dog. Apparently it was one of old Polly's puppies."

Beth took a deep breath. "Yes, I know. About the time Gail came here last year, Jim told me Hilda had promised them one without even asking him or Mum first."

"Well, now that you've been able to rent a house with a decent yard and not just a unit, is there any reason we can't take her home with us?"

Beth stood up. For a moment she wasn't sure what to answer. "Art, I'm not sure about having the dog, at least not yet. If I can get some work, I won't be home much to look after it, or keep it out of mischief."

Art looked up at her, his lips in a firm line. "I was going to tell you after this weekend. This leave has been kind of a trial run. The doctors told me if we cope okay, they think I'll be ready for discharge after another few days back in rehab. I just have to learn more about the exercises I have to do at home. I'll be able to help with the dog, especially after the kids go to school."

Utter delight and relief swept through Beth. "Oh, Art, really?"

He nodded, watching her closely.

She swooped on him, planting a kiss straight on his lips. "I'm absolutely thrilled. Why didn't you tell me before?"

He hesitated. She straightened, and her delight faded. Apprehension filled her as she saw the grimness in his face.

"Beth," he burst out with a trace of anger, "we'd been separated for over six months before the accident, and that happened a year ago now. We haven't talked about the way I left you. As I said last night, nothing's been resolved yet, and I—"

Deeply hurt, Beth drew back. "And you don't know if you want to continue with our marriage," she interrupted harshly.

"No, Beth, I wasn't sure if *you* really wanted me back. After all, it was me who walked out on you." She watched him swallow a couple of times before he continued. "I'm going to be less of a husband to you and a father to our children than I ever was. In fact all I'm going to continue to be is nothing but a burden and a bad tempered nuisance."

Beth drew herself up. "Arthur Canley-Smith, we did have some of this discussion before you agreed to be transferred from Sydney to Brisbane. It's a bit late to be changing your mind now," she flashed at him. "I left the kids all those months with Mum and Jim just to stay with you in Sydney. For goodness sake, they even had to employ Gail to help when Mum became so sick! I've now uprooted the children and myself, rented out our own house in Dalby, rented a house in Brisbane indefinitely to be near the best rehab available. The owner's even let us put in those special rails in the bathroom and bedroom, and that ramp for the wheelchair. What else do I have to do to prove to you that I want you home with us?"

"What else?" He was silent, looking down at his clenched hands. Then he looked up at her intently. After a long moment, he gave a strange little laugh. "I'm afraid I'll have to let you work that out for yourself, Beth, my dear."

three

Art sat perfectly still for a few moments after the flushed, bewildered face of Beth had disappeared.

Not once in all the dreary weeks and months since the accident had she told him she still loved him. Even if she had said the words he wasn't sure if he could believe them. Wasn't that the real reason he had driven off after that last dreadful fight? He had killed her love for him. If she'd ever really loved him. Besides, who could really feel a "death till we part" type of love for a man like him?

Even before they had been married, he had known she wanted him to be different from what he was. And for a while he had tried to be the kind of man she wanted him to be. He had tried his hardest to stop swearing when he realized how much she hated it. After all, with his strict upbringing that had been relatively easy. When she had said she hated him drinking, for years he had even stopped looking in at the pub for a beer on the way home from work.

Drinking! His lip curled. He'd never been much of a one for the beer anyway. It had been mainly the chance to spend a bit of time with his mates and relax after work. But she had never really believed that.

Things had deteriorated even faster between them after Robbie's birth. It had been bad enough before, but then he'd overheard that conversation between Beth and Jim. The murmur of voices from her room had reached him in the hospital corridor, and he'd paused, disappointed that once again someone was with Beth and he'd had so little time with her alone.

Then he'd heard Jim's concerned voice saying, "I know you now feel guilty about marrying an unbeliever, Beth, but Art's a great guy. You've got to hang in there. . ."

Guilty! Beth felt guilty for marrying him! He had gritted his teeth then as he did now at the memory. Everything had been religion's fault. It had denied him his parents, then it threatened his marriage.

Desperately hurt and feeling very insecure, he'd left the hospital without seeing Beth. In the weeks and months that followed he had spent more and more time away from the increasing tension at home, playing pool, playing cards, even playing the poker machines. Eventually, though, when he saw how seemingly levelheaded people put whole pay packets through them, he had steered clear of those.

The one thing he had firmly refused to do after Robbie had arrived was go to church with her again. Being in church, hearing familiar songs and sermons, had been torture. Besides Jim's words, it brought back bitter memories of his mother and father, whom he'd only seen that once since he was seventeen.

Sure, he'd been able to handle going to church occasionally when he and Beth first met, even more often after they were married. But boy! After Robbie had been born, Beth had nagged him more and more! The more she pestered him about religion, the more he had resisted. Nothing would have made him give in. She had treated him as though he was the biggest sinner around, but he could have told her about worse sins than a couple of low-alcohol beers a few times a week and some swear words. In fact, several times he would have loved to shock her religious socks off by telling her a few truths about his so-called very religious parents.

Of course, the final straw had been when he had lost his job as a heavy machinery mechanic because of the rural recession. And his employment dilemma still had not changed. In fact, it was worse now. Not only did he have no job and no income, now he couldn't even walk. Sure, moves were being made for him to be trained in a job that could be done from a wheelchair, but what woman would be prepared to put up with living on the poverty line indefinitely?

If only his parents had not kicked him out before he had finished senior high school. If only he'd been able to fulfill his ambition to go on to university instead of having to settle for a mechanics apprenticeship so he could earn some money to live on. If only. . . .

He moved abruptly and started wheeling his chair swiftly from the room. Very rarely did he allow the memories of his early years to rise up. They always made him feel as helplessly angry as he had all those years ago.

A small, miniature tornado tore out of a door and almost collided with him.

"Whoa," he exclaimed, "you shouldn't be running inside like that, Jacky!"

"What would you know? What do you know about anything!"

He gaped at her tear-stained, furious little face. Then his own hardened. "I know that I'm your father, young lady, and you don't speak to me like that," he started sternly.

"Why not?" the rebellious, tense little figure spat at him. "You might be my father, but you're never here, are you? You spoil all our fun! And you make Mum cry!" A sob tore out of the slight figure, and then she whirled away.

Art couldn't move. Anguish gripped him. He knew his little daughter had been very reserved around him, but he had never guessed she. . . .

"She hates me. . . ," he whispered out loud.

"Oh, no, she doesn't," the voice of his mother-in-law said softly from behind him. "She's hurt and bewildered, but she doesn't hate you. If you saw how she dwelt on every mention of you these past months, you'd know that."

He stared up at her silently, studying her sympathetic expression. "She's so wary around me. And I don't know how to talk to her anymore."

"You're almost a stranger to her, that's why," Mrs. Stevens said matter-of-factly. "Children grow up fast at her age, and you're just going to have to get to know each other again. Now," she added calmly, "I understand that you'll be leaving this morning, Art."

"Well," he said hesitantly, "that was what I thought best, but I take it Jacky hasn't taken too kindly to the idea." He sighed. "Perhaps Beth was right and we should leave them with you for the rest of the holidays."

"No," Mrs. Stevens said, "you're perfectly right in wanting them to go home with you. It's more than right that you want to spend time together trying to build up your family relationships again." Holding his gaze steadily, she said slowly, "When you're trying to build the bridges again, Art, would you make sure not to disregard the spiritual welfare of your family?"

His expression stiffened, and he looked away. "I leave all the religious stuff to Beth," he said gruffly.

"Mmmm, perhaps that's one of the reasons your marriage has been having such a rough time." Puzzled, he looked back at her. She was staring at him thoughtfully. "My daughter had a lot of head knowledge about. . .about 'religious stuff' as you call it, but I'm not too sure, until recently at least, she had much appreciation of what really living the victorious Christian life is about."

Art stared at her with a frown, not sure at all what she was getting at.

She smiled at him and then turned away. "If Will and I are going to get to church this morning, we'd better all get breakfast out of the way so you can leave," she tossed over her shoulder cheerfully.

By the time the car was packed and good-byes said, Art was immensely relieved to be getting away. He knew they were all disappointed except himself, and even he felt sad at leaving the beautiful, black-soil country. But being with the family again in such a way had brought too many reminders of how it had used to be.

Eons ago. At the beginning.

When Jim had befriended him at school. When he'd brought him home for visits and he'd caught a glimpse of what a loving family could be like. When he and Beth had started going together and taken long walks over the paddocks, talking, falling in love. When they had been married. When he'd been able to help Jim repair the farm machinery. When. . . .

At last Beth started the car. She glanced across at him with a cheerful, "I hope we've got everything. You okay?"

He nodded, and managed a smile that he tried to make as reassuring as he could. In fact, since the fall off his bed he'd had several bouts of pain when he moved a certain way. He had even asked his mother-in-law to give him some pain tablets when Beth had been busy somewhere else. Not for worlds would he worry her anymore.

Beth smiled gently back at him, and then they all waved their last good-byes.

"Bye Grandma! Bye Bonnie!"

Art winced at the mournful tones in Robbie's voice, feeling guilty again for being responsible for their leaving a day early.

Beth shot him another quick look and then set the car in motion down the track to the main road.

There was an unusual silence in the backseat. Art thought he heard a quickly muffled sniff and saw Beth glance in the rear vision mirror. She frowned.

Before she could speak, he said quickly, "Well, kids, how did you enjoy your first-ever wedding?"

Silence. Another sniff.

Desperately he tried again. "Did you manage to chuck those boxes of confetti onto Uncle Jim and Aunt Gail?"

"We don't call Gail aunt." Jacky's voice was subdued, but still a little belligerent. "She's just Gail. She said so."

At least it was some response, Art thought with a trace of amusement.

"I like Gail, and I throwed my stuff all over her." Robbie said. He sounded cross. "I do hate leavin' Bonnie."

"Threw your stuff," Beth corrected.

"Yes, I know! I threwed my stuff!" Robbie's voice sounded crosser.

Art stifled a chuckle. "As soon as those old doctors tell me I can come home for good, we're going to have to build a kennel for a dog, I suppose," he intervened quickly.

There was a brief silence. Then came a jumble of excited questions and comments from the backseat.

Beth glanced across and smiled at him. For a long time, Art found himself immensely cheered by the gentle approval that had been in her face. However, he was exhausted and in considerable pain by the time Beth at last pulled up in the driveway of the modest weather-board house in the northern suburbs of Brisbane.

Since the accident he'd learnt to hate car travel, even the short trip from the hospital to the house on weekends. It seemed to set off the muscle spasms in his legs, and sitting up for so long gave him a bad headache. The trip to the farm had been bad enough, but for some reason, the drive home set off more severe spasms than he could ever remember having, and once again his headache was a shocker. He was certainly paying for the trip to see Jim and Gail married!

He had not even thought of the problem that caused Beth to make a distressed sound when at last he rolled onto his side on the bed.

"Oh, Art, you've got a pressure sore," she wailed.

An expletive slipped past his lips before he could prevent it.

"It's no good swearing about it." Beth sounded exhausted and despondent. "I'm sorry. I should have insisted on rubbing your back more."

"It's not your fault," he growled. "I should know better myself. I'm supposed to change my position often to take the weight off. Let's hope it's improved by the time I go back to rehab."

"Well, there's quite a large red area and it does have a blister on it. Does this mean they might decide we can't manage well enough yet?"

She looked so upset, he forced a smile, "I shouldn't think so. It's not as though I'll be doing all this sitting in a car and a church every week."

&

To Beth's utter dismay, Art was wrong. The doctors did decide it was too soon for discharge.

By nighttime, Art had still been very pale. Beth had been bitterly disappointed when he looked at her with defeat in his eyes and said quietly, "You'd better ring up and tell them I'm coming back tonight."

Tuesday afternoon, Art told her gruffly that there was even more concern about the increased muscular spasms and bouts of pain than about the pressure area. The couple of bruises and the skin tear had also caused a few frowns.

"So it means they think I need more intensive training here in rehab than I'd get as an outpatient," he explained to Beth in short, clipped words. "They also want me to have a complete rest for a week. And they said to tell you it would be best not even to have visitors. Not even you," he added very firmly.

"Oh, Art!" Dismay and disappointment flooded through Beth. "You didn't do any damage when you fell did you?" she asked anxiously.

For one brief moment, he hesitated, but then he shook his head decisively and looked away. "Definitely not."

She looked at him helplessly. The children would be very disappointed, but a sudden, inexplicable feeling of relief made her feel guilty. Looking after him those few days had been a bigger strain than she'd expected.

She rushed to say as cheerfully as she could, "Oh, well, I suppose that will give the tradesmen more time to finish installing those extra rails in the bedroom."

Art's face tightened, and she knew that somehow he sensed her relief at the delay.

"Before I'm discharged, they want you to come in a few times and have more training in how to help me. Starting next week. In the morning." His voice was abrupt, and for a moment Beth thought he hesitated as though about to say something else. Then his lips tightened and he looked away.

Beth swallowed nervously, wondering how he was going to accept her news. "Art, I hope I won't need to be here Monday morning," she began hesitantly.

His eyes flew back to meet hers. He rapped out, "You

don't have to try and help me at all, Beth. I don't know how many times I've told you that."

Beth opened her mouth and then closed it again. The bitterness and resentment that blazed at her from his pale face shocked her. Months had gone by since he had let her see so clearly how he resented her having to help him.

"I've told you before. I can stay in this rehabilitation center until my third party insurance claim is finalized. Then. . ." He hesitated, looked away, and continued swiftly, "Then there should be enough money to employ a live-in nurse, and I could get a separate unit somewhere."

Despair rocketed through her. Her horrified gaze locked with his in shocked silence.

"Is that. . ." She swallowed on the hard stone in her throat, and tried again. "Would you really prefer that, Art?"

A strange look passed over his face, but he looked down too quickly for her to be quite sure what it had been. Tears blurred her own eyes, and it was her turn to look away. The fear that he still did not want to live with her was never very far from her mind.

"You and the kids would be a lot better off without a paralyzed man to care for, Beth." His voice was low and expressionless.

Beth's mouth went dry. The fear swept in on a relentless tide. Once again she opened her mouth, and then closed it without speaking. *Dear God. Think. Think quickly. Find the right words.*

She had so much she wanted to say. . .needed to say. But she had tried to say them before. Months ago. In Sydney he had not wanted her to arrange for his transfer, had not wanted her to be prepared to have him home. He had been silent then, too, just looked at her doubtfully, but he had not continued his protests about her looking after him, and she had tried to convince herself he had agreed. But now she knew she had only been kidding herself. All along, he. . .he. . . .

Art broke the heavy silence, his voice very low, "I need to be absolutely sure you want me home for more reasons than pity, Beth."

Somewhere deep inside her, a fervent, silent prayer went up. What could she say to convince him how much she needed him in her life? Surely he could never doubt that she loved him? Without him, the day were duller, the colors dimmed. . . .

She looked up from her clenched fists in her lap to see him watching her intently. That strange, intense look was on his face again. Suddenly it disappeared, leaving his expression carefully blank. She frowned, trying without success to see what he was thinking.

At last she stood up. Her legs were trembling so much, she held onto the bedside table to steady herself. He looked back at her, and she studied his closed face for a moment, failing, as she had many times before, to read what he was really thinking.

She took a deep breath, and was proud of herself when her voice came out steady and much stronger than her inward shaking indicated. "The children and I have had far too many months already to decide whether we'd be better off without you, Arthur Canley-Smith. All the time you. . . you've been gone we have not, I repeat, *not* been better off. I only asked if another time could be arranged because I have a part-time job interview that morning."

"A job interview!"

She lifted her head proudly. "Yes, with a friend of Reverend Telford. He has a small business near us. He needs help in the office Monday to Friday."

Art looked worried and angry. "But Beth, how are you

going to do that as well as look after the kids, and. . .me?"

He stopped abruptly, and after a moment she said softly, "I thought you would be able to help me a bit at home. And you do most things for yourself, Art. It's not as though you don't have the use of your hands like. . . ," she took a deep breath and continued, "like quadriplegics."

"That's right, I'm only a paraplegic, only paralyzed from the thoracic area down. I'm lucky, injury to the neck or lower back is much more common, the doctors keep telling me," he said sarcastically, and then added furiously, "*only* a paraplegic. We musn't forget that. And be thankful for small mercies, and all that garbage."

His explosive outburst made her take a step back. She had known a long time ago from others that he felt like this. But never before had he shown her the depths of his bitterness.

She breathed another silent, fervent prayer for the right words. Her instinct told her that the direction of their relationship depended greatly on the next few moments.

Beth stared back at him steadily, hoping he would see no hint of the dreadful ache that had closed on her heart. "Yes, Art, I am thankful you're not a quadriplegic. I'm also very thankful the doctors here believe you only have that Brown-Sequard Syndrome type of incomplete spinal cord lesion."

Art looked away, and she started to feel angry. While she had been afraid to talk about their marriage, he had refused to discuss his condition with her far too many times. She had been deeply hurt right at the beginning that he would never talk to her about the accident. She had even had to find out how he had really sustained his injuries from the police, Jim, and then much later from Gail.

Apparently Art had not actually been injured beyond a few bruises and cuts when the car smashed into his big interstate semi-trailer. A flying fragment of metal had been flung onto his back when the car's petrol tank had exploded. He had been found next to the unconscious Gail. Her severe injuries had not been consistent with his claim that she had been flung clear. Not until Gail had at long last visited him, and they had talked, had he admitted to dragging her from the car when he had seen the smoke and smelt the petrol. The grass fire that had been started by the explosion had set his clothes alight. If the rescuers had not reached him and Gail when they had. . . .

Beth shuddered. As it was, she couldn't bare to think of those dreadful burns that had for so long delayed any therapy and treatment for his back injury. Despite numerous skin grafts, there was still an ugly, deep, twisted scar in the middle of his back.

"One day you're going to be independent again, Arthur Canley-Smith." Beth did not know where the words came from, but even as they burst from her, she knew they were true. His eyes went swiftly to her face.

She glared down at him, and added with burning conviction, "The doctors in Sydney said you should be able to gain some use of your legs again. You may not be able to even walk the length of a football field again in one go, let alone run down one. But that's not going to matter a scrap. And I don't want you ever dare to believe differently. And I'm going to be there to see you do it. Every single, solitary step. . .of. . .the. . .way." She enunciated the last four words clearly and very loudly.

A startled look swept over Art's face. Then she saw utter amazement take its place. Beth felt a sense of satisfaction when it was his turn to open his mouth, and then close it again. His throat convulsed as he rapidly swallowed several times.

She couldn't bear any more. A stifled sob shook her and she swung away. She had reached the doorway, when his cracked, desperate voice stopped her.

"Beth darling, since when have I become Canley-Smith again? Isn't plain Smith good enough for you anymore?"

She stopped dead. He had called her darling. She couldn't remember the last time he had used any endearment to her.

Slowly she turned around. For a moment they stared at each other. Then an unwilling smile briefly tilted her lips with relief when she saw the teasing glint in his suspiciously bright eyes.

She straightened. "No, it's not good enough," she flung at him, "and at *our* wedding I married a Canley-Smith. Your real name is not plain Smith. You couldn't be plain anything if you tried!"

An expression she couldn't understand flashed across his face. "Oh, Beth. . ." His voice choked and he looked down, fiddling with the rug across his useless legs.

She waited patiently until he slowly raised his head. Then the unconcealed torment and fear in his face put wings on her feet. She was crouched beside him by the time the whispered words escaped him.

"Beth, what if you and those doctors are wrong? The doctors here have had grave doubts about my ever walking again after this long time lapse since the accident. What if I'm never able to be independent, except in a wheelchair, always needing someone, never walking again?"

Her hands crept up around his neck, slowly, fearfully, expecting the usual rejection of her touch. Suddenly he let his head drop against her, and with a tremendous sense of relief she cradled him against her heart.

"Then we will have to let God give us the strength day by day to cope," she whispered tenderly as she stroked his head.

"Day by day, Art sweetheart. We only have to cope day by day." She added fiercely after a tense moment, "But we will only be able to do it if we do it together. When I'm weak you'll need to be strong for both of us, and when you're weak, I'll be strong for both of us. But we will see it through together! With God's help, we'll see it through!"

For a moment Art was very still. Then a deep shudder went through him. But, for once, he did not argue or even comment.

four

Despite her confident words, an icy hand of fear settled deep inside Beth as she reluctantly left the rehabilitation unit and headed for the car-park. Her hands were trembling when she unlocked the car and scrambled inside. Helpless tears began trickling down her cheeks. Two clenched fists pounded on the steering wheel. Furious words burst from her. "I won't give up on our marriage, God! I won't, I won't!"

She knew what that scene had been all about. Art had been testing her, perhaps even trying to find an excuse not to come home and be with her, be with his family again. She had a horrible suspicion that he really did not want to see her or the children the next few days, that the medical staff had made no such dictate.

Impatiently she brushed away the tears, gritted her teeth, and started the car. The children had to be collected from school. Groceries had to be bought. She closed her eyes tightly for a moment, and cried out loud, "Oh, God! Oh, God. . .help. . .please help me!"

What if. . .what if she was wrong and Art was right? What if he never walked again? He had always put so much value in physical strength. Even at school, she had been aware of that when he had spent hours in the gym building up muscles, working out so he could be the best, the fittest in his football team.

As she set the car in motion, she muttered fiercely "He *will* walk. It has to be true. It must be true."

Saying the right words to Art had been easy enough. . .*let*

God give us the strength day by day to cope. But how would she cope with each day of uncertainty, with this other deep, inner fear. It was always there in the back of her mind: if there had been no accident, would Art ever have come home? Did he want to be with them now? Did he really want to stay married to her? Did he love her enough to really forgive her?

He had even been angry with the police and hospital authorities for contacting her as next of kin when he had been too ill to prevent them. Still, his bloodless, pain-wracked face had lit up that first day she had walked into his hospital room. But then he had shut her out, refused to talk to her about his condition. Any information about him she had to obtain from the medical staff.

Months after his burns had healed, when his paralysis had showed no real improvement, she knew the staff had been worried about his increasing depression. But with her he had always smiled, pretended everything "was fine, just fine." She had always known that the smile never reached his tormented eyes which he would so quickly hide. Oh, she had tried to talk to him. Tried to get him to talk to her, only to be met by a bland face, a raised eyebrow that all meant he would not let her near him emotionally.

The worst of his depression had lifted after Gail had gone to see him at long last. Beth wondered about that at times. She still wasn't quite sure what had happened that day. Jim had merely told her that Art had been relieved Gail no longer blamed him for the accident. But somehow she knew there was more to it all than that. And never through all the heartbreaking months had he ever let her get really close to him.

Until Saturday night when he had allowed her to cry all over him. Until today. Her heart lifted. For the first time he had briefly let _her_ comfort him. Even let her hold him close.

She was late picking up the children, and one look at their scowling faces made her heart sink. "Sorry, kids," she said brightly. "Hope you haven't been waiting too long."

"That's okay, Mum." Jacky's shrug and long-suffering voice made Beth search her face quickly. "I guess Dad held you up at the hospital."

"No, he didn't as a matter of fact." Jacky glanced at her and then away again. "It was very busy at the supermarket," Beth continued evenly. "The car-park was full and then there was a long queue at the cash register."

There was silence as she pulled out into the stream of traffic. She frowned slightly. Usually by this time Robbie was chattering away like a magpie.

"And how did your day at school go, Robbie?" she asked gently at last.

There was silence for a moment, and then a very subdued voice said, "Okay, I guess."

Beth opened her mouth, then bit her lip. She could find out what was wrong easier when she wasn't driving.

"Did the doctor tell Dad when he could come home again, Mum?"

Beth hesitated before answering her daughter. "I'm afraid they don't know yet," she said slowly at last. "In fact he needs a lot of rest to get over the trip to the farm. He still needs more training in how to manage at home."

She glanced quickly across at Jacky, but her daughter's head was turned away, hiding her expression. "Now," Beth added quickly, "when we get home, I need help putting my shopping away so we can see what we can do about a kennel for Bonnie."

"Why couldn't we have brought her back with us?" Jacky's voice was belligerent.

"'Cause when we went to school she'd be lonely durin'

the day, stupid!"

"Robbie, don't speak to your sister like that," said Beth sharply.

"Well, she is stupid." There was a sob in the shrill tones. "She said. . .she said Daddy's neva comin' home for good. She said—"

"Robbie! Shut up!" yelled his sister.

"Be quiet this minute," Beth exploded above Jacky's angry voice.

"But Mum—"

"Not another word until we're home!"

To Beth's relief, both children were silent the rest of the trip while she negotiated the heavy traffic. Crisply she demanded their help unloading the car. When the bags of groceries were safely in the kitchen, she rounded on them.

"Right. Let's get one thing very clear. Your father needs more time in hospital right now, but he is very definitely coming home for good once the doctor says he can."

Beth put her hands on her hips and glared from one to the other. Both children searched her face and then looked away. Robbie swallowed and Jacky's head bobbed down.

"Now, what's this all about?"

There was silence.

"Jacqueline. . . ," began Beth sharply.

Jacky raised her head and glared defiantly at her. "It's nothing, Mum. Robbie had a bit of a fight at school today."

"Robbie!"

Robbie glared at Jacky. "Dobber!"

Beth took a deep breath, but before she could speak, Jacky rushed in with, "It's not dobbing to tell your mother you had a bit of trouble at school. Mum told me when you first started school at Cecil Plains to look out for you."

"Jacky, telling tales is not what I meant about looking after your brother," Beth protested.

Two pairs of eyes considered her carefully. Jacky opened her mouth and then thought better of what ever she was going to say. Beth looked from her to Robbie. He was manfully fighting the big tears that had filled his eyes.

Suddenly those sad eyes looked so much like Art's that she couldn't think of a thing to say except a weak, "You kids want something to eat? I bought you some fruit."

Relief flooded Robbie's face as Jacky bounded away to scramble among the various plastic bags on the counter, calling "Great! Some white grapes. I love them."

Beth hesitated a fraction too long trying to decide whether to pursue what had happened at school. Robbie whirled away. He too grabbed a handful of grapes and the next moment both children had raced from the kitchen.

Annoyed with herself, Beth stared after them, and then sank wearily onto a chair. "You're a hopeless mother," she muttered under her breath. "When you were a kid, your mother would have had it out of you in a second!"

She bit a lip. Should she pursue it? Robbie in a fight? That wasn't like her young son at all. Like herself he did have quite a temper, but to her knowledge he had never hit anyone. Then she shrugged. At least his face had not been marked. The fight couldn't have been too bad, and after all, it was only early days at a new school. Some settling in problems were inevitable.

Resolutely she stood up. It was no good wishing her children could have kept going to the smaller country school on the Darling Downs that Jim, Hilda, and herself had attended before going to the senior high school in Dalby. Wearily she started stacking the groceries away.

Worry filled her as she remembered how much they had

cost. As usual she had spent too much money, and now there was barely any left until the next week's Social Security check. She dared not accept anymore help from Jim or her mother. Art would have a fit if he knew how much they had already helped out.

She found herself muttering out loud, "Oh, Lord, You know how desperately we need that job," and paused. She smiled slightly at herself.

"Practicing the presence of God" her mother had called it once. Beth had never done it before. But now, in the last few months, she found herself often talking to God spontaneously. Not only at odd moments either. She had spent many minutes on her knees in her bedroom when no one was around. Her one regret was that she had neglected having private devotional times during the years since she had married Art.

A sudden sense of peace came. She stood up and glanced around the small and rather dreary kitchen. For a moment she closed her eyes. "And You are here, aren't You?" she said out loud. "And You will give me strength each day."

"Mum? Who you talkin' to?"

Beth looked up. Robbie was looking around the kitchen with wide eyes. They settled back on her, and then suddenly lit with understanding. "Oh, that's what Grandma does. Can I have some more grapes?"

"If you say please," Beth answered automatically. "Grandma does what too, Robbie?"

"Talks to Jesus, of course."

Beth was still as he trotted off. Then she smiled.

❧

When the day of Beth's job appointment came, Rance Telford's friend greeted her with enthusiasm. She took an instant liking to him, but when she hesitantly asked if she could do his office work in the afternoon until her husband was out of the hospital, Bob Lane hesitated for a moment and her heart sank.

Then he shrugged. "Well, I was hoping you could answer the phone and do any reception work. I'm usually out doing jobs in the morning. But if it will only be for a couple of weeks I guess my wife could be here to do that." He beamed suddenly. "Our first baby's due in another few weeks and I—"

"And he wants me at home twiddling my thumbs until then," a cross voice said from behind Beth.

She turned and watched a tired-looking, pregnant woman stride slowly into the office.

"Beth Smith, is it? I'm Janet. I'll be very glad to have your help doing all the correspondence, invoices, and pays, but I can certainly sit and answer the phone and deal with visitors for a few hours each day." She settled on a chair with a sigh of relief, and then looked up and smiled at her husband. "At least, in the short term. Very soon I'll be too busy elsewhere for a while." She turned and surveyed Beth steadily. "Rance said you've just moved here to be near your husband's rehabilitation hospital."

"Actually, Art is expecting to be discharged soon." Beth took a deep breath. She hated putting it into words, but said steadily, "He. . .he's a paraplegic. I would normally have been able to come in at any time during school hours but. . .but they want me at the hospital to have some training in how to help him at home. It's so I can cope better with his daily care, exercises and things. The morning's best because of the showering and. . ." She faltered to a stop and looked away from the sympathetic understanding that had entered Janet's eyes.

"Well, now that you're here this morning," Bob asked a

little anxiously, "is there any chance you could work today for a few hours?"

His wife gave a snort of protest, but he said sternly, "Now, Jan, you know that you had a rotten night and should still be in bed. The doctor said your blood pressure's too high and that you've got to rest more."

"Don't. . .don't you need references or anything?" Beth asked unsteadily, relief flooding through her.

"Already have one from Rance," Janet Lane told her. "Oh, and he gave us strict instructions to ask you if you've found a church to worship at yet, and if not to invite you to come along with us to ours."

She grinned at Beth, and slowly, Beth smiled back. "Well, so far I've been too busy on Sunday mornings, either at the hospital or with Art at home. Perhaps later."

"Not too much later," warned Janet with a twinkle, "or the Reverend Rance will be after you."

Beth nodded in agreement, but as she drove to the hospital a few hours later, she wistfully wondered about going to church once Art was home. He had reluctantly gone to church with her from time to time until Robbie had been born. What would his attitude be now to her going regularly again?

Not seeing Art the last few days had been hard. She missed him dreadfully. She was determined that their visit today would be pleasant and cheerful, if nothing else, but when she strode into his room, she paused and exclaimed, "Art, You look dreadful. You're so pale and. . .and. . ."

"Don't fuss, Beth," he scowled, looking away from her. "I'm just back from working hard at physio, that's all." He added rapidly, "Now, tell me what your mother said about Bob Garret's funeral. You said on the phone that Jim and Gail were coming back for it."

Beth hesitated. She knew this was a ploy to stop her asking questions. He was always so reluctant to talk about himself!

"I shouldn't have let you and the doctors persuade me you needed rest and no visitors," she said crossly. "They've been working you too hard, and I would've told them so!"

"That's why they wanted me to rest after the sessions and not have to entertain visitors," Art snapped back. He glared at her. "Besides, you needed the break as much as me. Now, are you going to tell me about the family or not? How's Hilda?"

Gail sighed inwardly, but went along with him, trying not to let him see how anxious she was.

During the next few days her worry subsided as he gradually seemed less tired and strained. Her own days became increasingly hectic. In the morning she rushed to the hospital then managed usually to swallow a few mouthfuls of lunch before hurrying to work. She was careful never to be late again picking up the children. For a few days she had watched them closely, relieved when they appeared to have no further problems at school.

Art was not allowed home on leave again for several more weeks. He told her they wanted him to be more rested, and have uninterrupted physiotherapy. But something was different about him, and she was still secretly afraid he might have told them he did not want to go home. Jacky and Robbie willingly went with her a couple of times to see their father, but they quickly became bored in the hospital.

She was very tired by the time Art at last was again allowed a weekend leave. At first staying at home over the weekend without having to load the kids into the car and hang around the hospital was actually a relief. But then she found that looking after someone confined to a wheelchair was at times even more difficult than she had expected. Not that Art bossed her around or expected her to be at his beck and call every moment. Perhaps if he had been a bit less polite it would have been more natural? More normal? She just knew that he hated her doing things for him he could not do for himself.

But Beth refused to let him know how much his attitude hurt her. She gritted her teeth, muttered savagely to herself, "Day by day, Lord. Day by day," and kept smiling, although she was still fearful about how they would cope when he came home for good. More and more she found herself "talking to Jesus" and turning to her Bible. And more and more she began to experience the peace and daily strengthening she so desperately needed, especially when Art would be discharged.

five

"So, Monday's the big day, Beth?"

Beth looked up and smiled at Bob Lane. "Yes, it certainly is. And you're sure you can manage without me all day?"

"No problem." Bob smiled sympathetically. "Well, only another couple of days to go. We're not busy, why don't you leave a bit early?"

She returned his smile gratefully, grabbed her things, and fled. Janet and Bob Lane had become very good friends even though she still had not managed to take them up on their invitations to visit their church.

❧

Beth was filled with trepidation when she picked Art up on Monday. He was tense too, and gave one huge sigh as she drove carefully away from the entrance of the hospital. She glanced across at him, but he looked so grim she was silenced.

Neither spoke on the short journey home, and as she at last drove into their driveway and carefully stopped near the front ramp, she was once again battling her hidden fears. She sensed that Art was disturbed about his discharge.

He had been different lately. More abrupt. He had been so angry at her suggestion she have a good talk with his doctor before his discharge, that she had backed off.

Now she wondered if he was scared too. Did he think he would not be able to cope with being with her and the children again week after week? And could he cope with her helping him with the intimate things day by day he could not manage himself?

But at last they were home for good or ill. Turning off the motor, she took a deep breath and smiled determinedly across at Art.

He was staring through the windscreen at the house with such a strange look on his face that her smile faded abruptly. "Wouldn't it be lovely to be back in the country again, even in our own—?" Art's wistful voice cut off.

As nice as this house was, Beth had often thought the same thing after driving through the heavy city traffic. "The tenants in our house in Dalby want to buy it." Beth bit her lip. She hadn't intended to blurt it out like that. She had never found a good time to talk about their own home before. He had never seemed interested, but now Art looked at her swiftly and then away just as fast, but not before she saw the bleakness in his eyes.

She knew how he felt. They had battled so hard to get the deposit to put down on their own home. Now, even with the rent income, it was very hard keeping up the mortgage payments. Having to sell was a distinct possibility.

Without another word, she opened her door and went to unload the wheelchair. By the time she had unfolded it and wheeled it to the passenger side, Art had his door open and was swinging his legs, one by one, out of the car. When he was settled into the chair, she hurried ahead, leaving him to slowly manoeuver it up the ramp. Still without a word, she inserted her key in the lock, flung back the door, and waited.

Art paused and for a heart-stopping moment stared up at her. "I'm not sure that I ever really believed this wonderful day would come," he whispered at last. "I can unpack and I won't have to leave again after only one night."

Relief swept through her on a cleansing tide. Before she could speak, a faint grin twisted his lips and he said in a stronger voice with a hint of self-derision, "I feel a bit like the first time we arrived home after our honeymoon."

Her eyes blurred at the sudden vivid memory. They had both been so young, still teenagers, nervous and excited at the same time. And they had both been so much in love.

"For me to carry you over the threshold this time, you'd have to sit on my lap."

She searched his face for a moment, but there was nothing in his expression now except jubilation and amusement. Her heart lightened.

A relieved laugh escaped her. "That might be safer than hauling me over your shoulder in a fireman's lift, then dumping me on the floor as soon as you took two steps inside."

"Let's see shall we?"

Before she could do any more than gasp, he reached up, grabbed her by the arm, and pulled her down across him.

"Art! You. . .you idiot. . ."

She squealed and grabbed for support as his hands left her. The wheelchair bounced forward. One of her legs bumped against the door frame and she was jolted back against him. She squealed again, but they stopped moving. Two strong arms came around Beth again. She tightly clasped Art's neck.

For a moment she revelled in their closeness. Then his arms pushed her away slightly before letting go. Reluctantly she took her hands from his neck and bounced to her feet. She bent over and rubbed at her foot. "Ouch, that hurt. And that was even less graceful than your first attempt, Art Smith!"

She looked up at him, and all laughter fled.

"Not the most sensible thing either," he gasped breathlessly. "You're heavier than I thought."

"Oh, Art, you've hurt yourself!"

He shook his head. "Just winded" he managed.

"Are you sure? Are you in pain? Can I get you anything?"

"Don't. . .fuss. . ."

She stared at him anxiously. His chest was heaving. Those hazel eyes were closed in a face that had lost color, and his hands were clenched in his lap. Nervously she crouched down and put her own hand hesitantly over his and waited.

After a few moments, his breathing eased. He opened his eyes and looked at her. "Worse than the last time, huh?"

Not sure what to say, she stared back at him silently.

Something sparked in his eyes as they looked at each other. "But it was worth it. Like the last time," he murmured.

Art loved the way Beth's smile started in her eyes and then spread all over her face. He could not resist reaching up and tracing her smiling lips. Then it seemed his hand had a mind of its own as he reached around her head and tugged her closer.

"Last time. . ." he felt her lips move against his and then they were still as his silenced them.

Even as he kissed her, Art knew it was a mistake. It would only make it more difficult resisting his burning desire to hold her so close they would never be separated again. But for years he had tried so hard to be the kind of man she needed, and his best had never been good enough. He had an even better reason now not to let her get too close to him: his useless body. And last year he had reached the heights of cowardice. If Gail had not visited him at just the right moment. . .He shuddered.

And now these last few weeks. . . .

He took a deep breath, wondering once again at himself. Why hadn't he been able to tell her? Why had he even gone so far as insist that the doctor and staff not say a word?

Beth straightened and looked at him with a slightly dazed expression.

He avoided her eyes and said as lightly as he could, "Let's get my gear in from the car and unpack."

You fool, he chastised himself silently. *Why on earth did you go and kiss her like a starving man?* His lips twisted at the obvious answer. He *was* a starving man, starving for her love, her acceptance. . .her. . . .

But as Beth moved away, there was a glow of happiness about her that he could not regret. Having a bit of foolish fun like hauling her onto his lap had felt good. The past years had been so serious, so worrying.

A few moments later Beth returned with his bags and walked toward his bedroom. He wheeled himself slowly after her, his thoughts and emotions still in turmoil, hoping she did not know how much that kiss had affected him. She hesitated in the middle of the room, looking at him expectantly. He glanced around the room casually.

Then he stilled, staring at the huge, slightly lopsided sign taped on the wall above his bed. "Welcome home, Dad," he read out loud. A sudden mist blurred his eyes.

"Jacky insisted on printing the words and then they fought over who colored it in," Beth said softly.

He cleared his throat. "They're good kids."

"Most of the time."

There was a wry note in her voice, and he looked sharply at her. "They been playing up on you?"

Beth was biting on her lip. He knew that habit of old. She had blurted out something she did not want him to know about. He was even more sure of it when she said a little too quickly "No, no, they're fine."

"Beth." He paused, and then added carefully, "We have to work out ways I can be of use around her. And one of them is sharing the responsibility of the kids. Especially while you have to work." Her head reared back, and he added rapidly, "It's all right, I know the kids have to get to know me a lot better again before I can come any of the heavy father bits. Your mother has already pointed that out to me."

Beth frowned, but turned away without speaking.

"What's wrong, Beth?"

"They. . .the kids. . ." Beth paused and then swung around. She looked troubled, and then blurted out "They're really excited about you coming home for good. I had a real battle to get them to go to school this morning, but I think they're also a bit scared about all the changes in their lives lately. You'll have to be very patient with them for a while, Art."

"I'm very much aware of that, Beth."

"I. . .I don't won't you to be hurt by them."

Art felt all his breath leave him in a whoosh. She was worried in case they hurt *him*! And he had been so worried in case he upset them.

Then he remembered the hurt that had clutched him after Jacky had flared at him after the wedding. More recently, he had been aware that Robbie had taken to being very careful around him. And he had discovered that seeing his son scuttle out of the room the moment he realized he was alone with his father had affected him badly.

He forced a smile at Beth's anxious face. "I'll be fine. I promise. Besides, didn't you say Jim and Gail were bringing the dog this coming weekend?"

Beth's face cleared. She raised her eyes to the ceiling and back. "I'm not sure I've forgiven Jim yet for letting the kids have that puppy of Hilda's," she grumbled.

"Gail assured me she has house-trained it."

"There's no way it's going to be living in the house," Beth stated firmly.

But Robbie and Jacky had different ideas.

Art watched with considerable amusement the next weekend as their insistent faces and voices at last wore Beth down to a feeble "We'll wait and see."

"Okay, kids, outside and play with Bonnie now," Art said firmly, trying hard not to laugh.

As the children raced away, a wildly excited collie dog barking happily after them, Beth looked at him ruefully. "Don't you dare say a word, Arthur Canley-Smith!"

Jim gave a wicked chuckle. She turned and glared at him.

"Don't take any notice of them, Beth," her new sister-in-law said. "Those two little imps twist their uncle around their little finger. . .well, at least they did when it came to having one of Polly's puppies. Oh. . ." Her smile disappeared. "Beth, did your mother tell you about Polly?"

Beth shook her head. "Not a word. Why, what's happened?"

Gail hesitated, and Jim said slowly, "Polly had cancer in the nose and Hilda had to have her put down."

"Oh, no, poor Hilda! She really loved that dog," said Beth sadly. "And so close to losing her father! How is she?"

Jim swept his hand through his hair and frowned. "I'm not really sure. Jean Drew stayed with her as long as possible, and Rance Telford has been keeping an eye on her since. But she's gone off to Sydney with him. We're a bit worried about her, both of them in fact."

Art snorted. "She'll be okay with the Rev. He of all people should be able to stop her making more mischief."

"That's all over, Art." Gail's chin was tilted and her voice firm. "God's dealt with her about the trouble she caused between me and Jim. We're going to be good friends from now on. In fact, I'm real pleased you've got Bonnie.

Perhaps one day she'll have puppies and you can give one to Hilda."

Beth noticed a strange look cross Art's face as he watched Gail. "But then, you'd forgive anybody anything, wouldn't you Gail?" His voice was soft, but filled with admiration.

Beth looked sharply from him to Gail.

Color swept into Gail's face. She tilted her chin and looked Art straight in the eye. "Only because I know that Jesus has already forgiven me. . .forgiven me and made me a new person."

Beth's eyes widened. She looked nervously at Art. He had been so rude to Rance Telford when he visited him during one of his first weekend leaves at home that she expected some kind of explosion.

For a moment there was a very thoughtful expression on Art's face. Then he scowled. Beth opened her mouth, but paused when a twisted grin eased his face.

"How come you've learned to talk so much like Jean Drew, the dragon lady, so quickly?" There was disgust in his voice. "These religious Stevenses and their friends have really got to you, haven't they, Gail?"

"Arthur!"

Gail ignored Beth's exclamation. "It's the Lord Jesus that has 'got' to me, Art Smith. And He could transform your life too if you'd let Him! You need Him in control of your life now more than you ever have."

Beth held her breath. So many times when she had tried to talk to Art like this before their separation, he had bitterly resented it. She looked helplessly at Jim. He was grinning madly at her!

"Don't look so appalled, sister dear. These two carried on like this quite often in Sydney when you were back home with the imps!"

"They did!"

For a brief moment, Beth felt a streak of jealousy. Why did Art tolerate this from Gail and not her?

Jim unconsciously answered her. "He listens to her because she was almost as big a heathen as he still is!"

Art gave a slightly forced laugh, and Beth looked away. She bit her lip. That had been one of the many accusations she had hysterically flung at him over the years.

"Jim Stevens, I was never a heathen," protested Gail with a grin.

Jim stood up. He grinned back at her. "Oh, yes you were, sweetheart. My dictionary says a heathen is an irreligious person, or even more specifically, not a Christian, and you were sure that. The very first time we met you took great pains to tell me you weren't at all interested in finding out about God."

Beth watched Gail's lovely face break into a rueful smile as she too remembered.

"What made you change your mind, Gail?"

Three heads swung toward Art.

He scowled. "Well, something must have happened. I've often wondered. And I don't think I really fit your definition of a heathen either, James!"

"Mmm. . ." Gail's voice was thoughtful. "You've certainly not given me the impression you're uninterested in God. At least. . ." she hesitated, "at least not for a long time. But you've never let me talk about my commitment to Christ before, Art. Are you sure. . . ?"

"Wouldn't have asked if I wasn't interested."

Beth again held her breath at the snarled words, but Jim laughed. "I hope you know what you've let yourself in for, Art, my friend. Once you start this wife of mine going on about her conversion, you might find it hard to stop her. I'll go and rescue Bonnie from the imps and leave you to it. Coming, Beth?"

Beth hesitated. Then she said slowly, "No, I'd rather like to hear what Gail has to say myself. I've never really heard what happened either."

She saw the smile exchanged between her brother and his wife before he disappeared, and her own heart ached. She had never known that same depth of intimacy with Art. Never. Not even in those first halcyon days of their marriage.

"Art, before we talk about all that, I haven't said anything about. . .about. . ."

Beth looked sharply at Gail as her voice choked to a stop. She was looking at Art hesitantly. Then she raised her chin decisively and said rapidly, "I'm so glad the coroner's report completely cleared you of any responsibility for the accident. And I'm so sorry I ever thought differently."

Beth gasped. "The report's out! Oh, Art, why didn't you tell me?"

Art avoided her eyes. He had hoped Gail wouldn't mention it until he'd been able to pluck up the courage to show it to Beth. To his utter amazement the coroner had highly commended his efforts to pull Gail from the burning car moments before it had exploded.

"It arrived last week," he growled roughly. "I didn't want to talk about it." He glared at Gail. "Thought I told you a long time ago to shut up about all that sorry business. Now what about this so-called conversion of yours?"

He risked a glance at Beth's face, and winced inwardly. He'd hurt her again, no matter how much she was trying not to let him see. But the report had stirred up all the horror, and he had not been able to bring himself to show it to her.

He deliberately looked back at Gail. She was studying him carefully, and then she smiled at him understandingly.

"You know, I've given a lot of thought to why I first began to take Christianity seriously." Gail propped her chin on her hand. She stared blindly in front of her with a far away look in her eyes. Then she looked up at Art and grinned a little shyly. "You were partly right you know, Art."

He quirked an eyebrow at her with mock indignation. "Of course I'm usually totally right. But which great thing am I. . .er. . .only partly right about?"

He gave Gail a mock scowl, and then glanced suddenly at Beth's uncertain smile and grinned gently at her. He thought her return smile held considerable relief.

Gail laughed and then sobered quickly. "You were right about the Stevens family and their friends. I guess it started with Jean Drew."

Art watched her expression soften as she thought of the nursing sister who had once been her clinical nurse educator at the hospital where Gail had done most of her practical nurse's training.

"I didn't realize until I was in the hospital after the accident how much she had changed from the bitter, sarcastic woman we were all scared of during our training. She was wonderful to me during those weeks when I was confined to bed," Gail added softly.

Art thought of the gray-haired woman who had also visited him often. She had always been there for him, as well as for Beth, during many dreary weeks after the accident.

"Yeah, she's an okay lady," he admitted gruffly.

"It wasn't until Jim mentioned how different she was now she'd become a Christian, that I realized what had changed her so much. Then. . ." she paused, and looked at Beth with a smile, "then I lived round the clock with two very committed Christians like your mother and brother. Gradually it sunk in that their faith and commitment to Jesus Christ touched every aspect of their lives.

"It wasn't that going to church every Sunday and being involved in their church life was just their particular life-style, like others I've known. I soon realized it was all far more than that. They weren't perfect, they just enjoyed God. There was a quality of love toward each other and others that I'd never seen so consistently before. There was peace and a joy too, and I desperately needed it all. And what's more they didn't have to do anything in their own strength. They just knew God worked out for good everything that happened in their lives."

Art looked at Beth and caught her eye. He stared at her thoughtfully, remembering what she had said. The color rose in her cheeks and she suddenly looked down at her clenched hands. He scowled. Now what on earth had Gail just said that had upset her so much?

There was a burst of furious yapping outside. Gail paused, and then she shrugged and stood up. "I guess what I'm try-ing to say is that they never doubted for a moment that God loved them, no matter what. After I asked her, Jean explained about the proof of God's love for all time being that He sent Jesus to die for me. I found I just couldn't turn my back on that kind of loving, and so I asked God to forgive me, and take control of my life and. . ."

The noise of kids and dog drew closer.

". . .And despite all the hassles since then, life's been. . . been great ever since," she finished rapidly.

As the kids rushed into the room with the dog barking at their heels, Art saw a radiance in Gail's face that he had only ever seen there when she mentioned her faith in Christ.

For a moment, depression rolled over him like a dark

cloud. A lovely woman like Gail would have no problem getting close to God. She had once urged him to do the same when he had been in the depths of despair at his injuries. He had heard what Beth had said numerous times over the years about Jesus Christ loving him. . .dying for him. He hadn't believed her then, and he just couldn't believe Gail now.

Of course God loved good people like the Stevenses and Gail. But how could God possibly love a man like him? Someone who could never even please his own parents. Someone whose own mother and father hadn't been able to love or forgive. Someone who had deliberately turned away from God time after time.

And now. . . .

How could he consider for one moment crawling back to God when he was such a helpless, incapacitated half-man?

"Daddy! Uncle Jim said ta ask you if we can use some old stuff under the house to build a dog's kennel for Bonnie."

"Robbie! I told you Mum said I could use that for a cubby house!"

Art stared at his two children, both racing toward him, jostling each other, trying to get closest to him, pleading eyes and voices trying to get his attention. Just so had they run to him numerous times over the years when they were much smaller.

But not for a long, long time. And certainly not this last week. They had been so careful around him. It had been "yes, Daddy, no, Daddy" until he'd actually wished they had been horrible to him.

Beth stood up. He looked up at her over their heads and their eyes clung. She had been as aware as he of Jacky and Robbie trying to be perfect children.

He knew the lump in his throat would betray him if he

tried to speak. Ashamed of his unexpected burst of emotion, he swallowed, and stared at Beth helplessly. She moved swiftly toward him. Then he felt her hands settle gently on his shoulders and his heart swelled with love.

"I said some of that junk under the house might be handy, Jacky." Her voice was very firm. He felt her hands tighten. "Your father can't be expected to make a decision until he knows what you're on about. Let him go and have a look first, and than he can help Uncle Jim sort you terrors out."

He put up a hand and grasped one of Beth's. Immense gratitude flooded through him. She was reestablishing him in his role as father. He glanced up, and her smile was so gentle, so beautiful, his heart ached.

He cleared his throat. "Okay, kids, what about you help me manoeuver outside and let me see what you're on about? Sounds like that uncle of yours needs all the help he can get."

Robbie hesitated, but Jacky surged forward. Beth stood back and let her grasp the handles of Art's chair. Gail moved to stand beside Beth and together they watched the trio disappear from the room.

Then Beth looked across at Gail. "Oh, Gail. . ." she began helplessly.

Gail gave a slight sound and quickly moved to put her arms around Beth. "Beth, dear, it's going to be fine. God hasn't let either of us survive that dreadful accident without many reasons. And Art has changed so much since the first day I met him. Why, just then he actually asked me about my becoming a Christian!"

Beth hugged Gail briefly, and then stepped back and mopped at her eyes. "Gail, I'm so ashamed. While you were talking about what a witness Mum and Jim were to you, I knew that my own Christian witness was far too many times practically nonexistent as far as Art was concerned. Especially after Robbie was born, I was always tired, and I. . .I used to lose my temper at the drop of a hat. I said some awful things to Art. I nagged him so much. . .about going to church with me, even about becoming a Christian."

"A bit like a dripping tap, you might say?"

Beth smiled weakly. "Yeah, guess I was a real example of that verse in Proverbs. My dear Mum's already pointed that one out to me, and also the one about a wife winning her husband by her behavior *without* talking at him." She straightened. Her head went up. "So, no more words from me," she said firmly. "Just prayer. Each day, just prayer, and more even for myself than Art."

"Yes," said Gail slowly, "prayer is vital. But sometimes the right words do have to be said at the right time—God's time. I'm also finding out how much I need fellowship and worship with other Christians. Some days I still miss my family so much." She took a deep breath. "But spending extra time on those days reading and meditating on the scriptures always helps. Especially when I'm prepared to put what I learn into practice," she added with a rueful smile.

Her words pierced through Beth. So few times over the years had she found strength in the Bible like that. She knew so much about what was in it. Her parents had seen to that. But how little during her marriage she'd consistently read, studied, made it a vital part of her life.

She walked across to the window and looked out on the backyard. Jim was standing talking to Art, while Jacky and Robbie were carrying a piece of timber toward them.

"You're right, Gail," she murmured. "Mum always said it contains God's instructions for living. That even includes instructions for praying." Her voice firmed. "I'll do better from now on."

She turned around slowly, and the two women smiled at each other.

six

"Art, is there anything else—?"

"No, I'm fine. Just get going, woman!"

Art knew his voice had been too abrupt, and he forced a smile at Beth's worried face.

"Just go, Beth, or the kids will be late for school. I can ring you if anything goes wrong. And you'll be home before the hospital car comes to take me to physio."

Beth frowned. "I still think it's strange that they suddenly decided you needed to go every day. You're so tired after those sessions. And anyway, why couldn't I pick you up in the afternoons after work?"

"Because you'd be too tired running me around every day as well as timing it all with the kids. Because the hydrotherapy takes ages. Because some days they may be able to bring me home earlier than others. Besides," he continued grimly, "the hospital car had to be booked on a daily basis, some stupid red tape, hospital rules or something. And because the doctor said three short sessions were not enough to strengthen my muscles." There was a bite in his voice, and Art once again forced himself to grin at her carefully. "Can't be helped," he added breezily, "the powers that be did dictate, and we obey." He felt immensely relieved when she pulled a wry face, glanced at her watch, and headed for the door.

Art spotted something on the table. He picked it up and hurriedly wheeled after her. "Is this somebody's lunch box?" he called.

Beth gave an exasperated snort and flew back. "Jacky's. Thanks." She grabbed the box, kissed him unexpectedly on the lips, and disappeared out the door.

Art touched his mouth. The kiss had been so natural, so spontaneous. He wheeled himself out the front door so he could wave them off, and his heart glowed when Jacky grinned at him and waved enthusiastically. Robbie, however, only glanced at him quickly and then looked away.

As the car disappeared from sight, a feeling of something like relief swept through Art. He was glad to be alone at last after the weekend. Come to think of it, this was the first whole morning he'd been really alone since the accident last year. This was heady stuff! Now he could choose how to spend the next few hours without being told what to do by some nurse or therapist or doctor.

Silence descended around him for a blissful moment. Then Bonnie gave a short, sharp bark from the backyard where she had been banished. "Well, alone except for one collie dog," he muttered.

The winter day was quiet and sunny. Too soon the cold winds would sweep in, and even subtropical Brisbane would be cold for a few weeks. The breeze that had sprung up was a little cool, but suddenly Art was reluctant to leave the porch. He had spent far too much time indoors these past months.

Bonnie barked again, and then whimpered. "Why not?" Art muttered.

He wheeled the chair down the ramp and around to the side gate into the backyard. The lawn was too soft in places for the narrow wheels on his chair, but fortunately there were plenty of sidewalks around the house.

The collie greeted him with delighted yelps. With some difficulty, Art managed to reach up and release the catch on the high gate. Bonnie pushed her way forward, and he just managed to stop her squirming past him and out of the yard.

"Oh, no you don't, you wretch. You're not going to get away from me and give young Robbie something else to be unhappy with his father about." He managed to grab the dog's collar, and hang on until he had moved his chair inside far enough that he could close the gate. "Not real bright, Arthur. You could have lost the dog your first morning alone, and then so much for your assurances that you can cope!"

Art frowned, thinking of the last week. When he had been discharged, it had been arranged that Beth would take him to his physiotherapy sessions at the hospital. The only appointments available for Mondays, Wednesdays, Fridays had been in the early morning.

Fortunately Beth had been able to continue working for Bob and Janet Lane each afternoon after school that first week home. But it had been with the proviso that his appointments would be switched to the afternoon as soon as possible so she could work the mornings. He knew she had been worried about what would happen if he could still not get afternoon appointments when Janet could no longer work. So, at his session last Friday, he had again asked if there was a vacancy yet in the afternoon appointments. His physiotherapist had looked at him thoughtfully, and then muttered something about talking to his doctor.

The two professionals turned out to have already had considerable discussion. They had decided that he needed to continue to have daily therapy.

"We probably should readmit you, Art," the doctor said hesitantly. "You insist you can't, or won't do. . .er. . .certain exercises at home, and only three sessions a week is proving not to be enough to ensure the progress we hoped for."

"No! There's no way I want to be readmitted." Art saw the doctor's lips tighten at his vehemence, and added hastily, "Surely there's some other alternative. I don't want to disappoint Beth and the kids. Or me, for that matter," he pleaded wistfully. "I've been in the hospital so long already. What about the hospital transport?" He swallowed, and continued rapidly as he saw the doubtful looks on their faces. "Isn't there any way you could arrange appointments and transport, even if it does mean I have to spend more time here waiting for them to take me home?"

Art suspected that his doctor and the physio had worked hard persuading the powers that be that he needed special consideration. The end result had been that the only way they could fit him in was to call for him late in the morning, and take him home when they could in the afternoon. He knew Beth had been immensely relieved, although she had been worried about his need to go every day and the length of time he would be gone.

But as things turned out, she'd had a phone call over the weekend from a worried Bob Lane. In an attempt to try and control her blood pressure, Janet had been confined to bed by the doctor. They needed someone to work from nine until three. If Beth couldn't do it, they would have to find someone else.

Beth had bit her lip when she told him, then glanced at him apologetically as she hurried on to say how fortunate it was the change in his schedule had already been arranged.

He had really enjoyed his first full week at home, he thought now, as he stroked the dog. Oh, sure, there had been moments of tension between Beth and himself; the hardest thing for Art had been the children's attitude to him.

He had been relieved to have Gail and Jim visit for several hours last Saturday. For far too brief a time, Jacky and Robbie had seemed to accept him while he and Jim had started erecting the wooden shelter that was part cubby house, part large doghouse. But yesterday the two children had been very quiet and avoided being alone with him again, especially Robbie.

Art wheeled over and studied the rough construction they had worked on. Old paving bricks had been put on the ground, and the walls made from old timber found under the house. An old tarpaulin temporarily adorned the roof. Jim had promised faithfully to bring some old pieces of roofing iron and more timber from the farm on his next visit.

"Hope the cold westerlies stay away until he gets back," Art said out loud, "or you'll be cold if that tarpaulin flies off, Bonnie old girl."

Bonnie whimpered, and he felt her long nose nudge under his arm. He chuckled softly and patted her again. "Missing the kids already, are you?"

With a sigh the dog rested her head on his knees, and they enjoyed each other's company for a while, Bonnie lost in some doggie world, and Art thinking about building the shelter. His lips twitched as he remembered the overenthusiastic help from the children. But Jim had dealt with them all calmly and efficiently.

Then he frowned a little. He knew that Jim had been careful to build the shelter next to the wide garden path so it would be accessible to the wheelchair. It still troubled him that the best spot would really have been against the back fence under a spreading poinciana tree.

Then he shrugged. It had been worth it. Jim had also been

careful to make sure Art had been included as much as possible in the building, handing him a hammer and a bunch of nails with the laughing comment, "Just because you can't reach the higher bits doesn't mean you get out of all the work."

He had noticed Robbie look at Jim with a wide-eyed stare, and then back at himself. Perhaps one day Robbie too might realize that his father wasn't completely useless.

Jim's attitude had been so typical of his brother-in-law. He was a fine man, and he and Beth had always been very close. Art had accepted years ago that he would never be able to measure up to a man like Jim, especially in Beth's eyes.

Seeing his old mate so happy with his new wife was great, though, and if anyone deserved to find happiness after so much tragedy in her life, it was Gail.

They weren't perfect, just enjoyed God.

Gail's words had crept back into his head constantly since Saturday. He did not know what had got into him. Fancy actually asking her to talk about her religion. No, he corrected himself with a snort, "religion" wasn't apparently the right word. Once before, when they'd first met, she had pointed out to him she wasn't just religious, she was a Christian.

At the time he had mentally placed his ultra-strict parents most definitely in the "religious" category. Their rigid attitude to going to church, keeping the Ten Commandments, and a host of other do's and don'ts had been so different from Gail's—and the Stevenses', come to that.

His frown deepened. Enjoy God? How on earth could anybody "enjoy God"? He doubted if even a saint could enjoy the God of wrath and judgement his parents had believed in!

As always, he deliberately blanked out any thought that

included his parents. He swung his wheelchair around so abruptly he bumped into Bonnie. She let out a yelp and ran.

He stopped, held out his hand, and called to her. "Oops, sorry girl. Come on, I won't hurt you again. Someone always gets hurt when I think about my parents." The bitter thought came, *Usually me*, but he pushed it away and called to Bonnie again.

The dog hesitated. Then she seemed to make up her mind he wanted to play. She gave a short bark, put her head down low between her front feet, and then with another playful yap pranced toward him. He gave a low chuckle when she dodged his hand, and took off around the yard. She paused again. With her tail wagging madly, she crept paw by paw closer and closer. Then, with her head down again, she woofed pleadingly at him.

Art found himself laughing at her. He moved his chair abruptly toward her and she took off again, this time racing round and round the rotary clothesline. "You win, Bonnie," he called.

Then he sobered. He'd never be able to chase a dog in a playful mood as he had once. Suddenly his chin went up. But there was no reason he wouldn't be able to chase one somehow, even if it had to be in a wheelchair.

"You wait until I build up my muscles, dog," he said fiercely. "Even if my legs never work properly again, I'll still get about somehow. I'll still chase you, even if it has to be in one of those new motorized expensive wheelchairs!"

Then he stopped. It was the very first time he had verbalized his intention not to allow his useless legs to limit him. A weight suddenly rolled off him.

Okay, so he did not have the legs he'd once had. That didn't mean he could not learn different ways of doing things. His time in rehab had certainly emphasized that.

They had assured him he'd even be able to drive a specially adapted car one day. Not one of the huge transport trucks perhaps, but certainly a car.

He looked at the kennel-cubby house again. He had managed to hammer those nails very straight and very effectively. He thought about all the skills for looking after himself that the therapists had been trying to instill in him. Most he was already handling quite well at home.

But the biggest decision still had to be made. What kind of work should he now attempt? What kind of training should he now have? How could he again support his family? Should he seriously consider that suggestion by the occupational therapist about doing some computer course at the Adult Education College? He had never had any chance to learn much about computers, but they had always intrigued him.

Some deep masculine pride inside him had been hurt when Beth had told him about her job, even though it certainly eased their financial difficulties. He had not minded at all her working while he had been also employed—but he felt different now that he and their rest of their family were dependent on her income.

Then Art thought about that for a moment. He took a deep breath. Honesty time. He had to admit it. True, he had never minded her working, but he had minded her earning more money than himself. He had been very relieved when the second baby had arrived and she had stopped work altogether.

Another thought suddenly hit him. After Robbie had been born she had mentioned a few times something about getting a part-time office job. He had been earning plenty himself then and he had dismissed the idea carelessly. Had he been wrong? She had always enjoyed working.

During the months away from Beth, he had finally decided she had become such a pain because of her guilt at marrying him, even more because of her guilt at letting him seduce her so they'd had to marry because she'd been pregnant. He had often wondered if she'd ever have ended up marrying him except for the baby.

But had he been wrong? Had being stuck at home with another baby contributed to her cranky moods? Perhaps that was why she had seemed to always be going out to something at the church, until he'd felt as though he and the kids were being neglected. At the time he had been secretly furious with her, thinking she was becoming too much like his mother, always plenty of time to bake cakes for church suppers and church sick folk but with hardly ever any time left for her family.

Deliberately, he forced his attention away from the past and thought again about the future. He had to do something to earn an income, to support his family. Well, he could never go back to being a specialized mechanic on the big machinery again. Climbing over and under tractors, harvesters, even driving a truck were no longer options.

He shut his eyes tightly for a moment, fighting to get rid of the negative thoughts. A wave of weariness washed over him.

He had not slept very well last night. Perhaps he had been overtired, but after falling into a brief, deep sleep, he had then lain wide awake for hours worrying about his relationship with Beth, about getting closer to Robbie, about what the doctor had told him, about the future, and then of course, like a nagging toothache, he had not been able to get Gail's words about God out of his head.

A sudden longing for the faith and the peace she so obviously had found swept through him. "Are You as real as she and the Stevenses think, God? Are You really different from what I grew up thinking You must be like? Was everything *they* told me about You lies?" he muttered out loud. "Do You really care about miseries like me?"

He sighed wearily. He really didn't need these thoughts about God creeping in all the time. He had enough day-by-day things to worry about.

One thing he had not expected his first week home was the fact that he would get so very tired still. He knew his tiredness was probably caused by a combination of longer hours out of bed and not having nurses at his beck and call. But above all, the emotional tension between himself and the children, and between himself and Beth exhausted him.

One day at a time, so many people had told him, the doctors, nurses, occupational therapists. One day at a time.

And Beth had brought God into that idea. She sure believed that He was this "day-by-day" thing's very source of strength. His heart softened. Beth was sure some woman.

She always had been of course, but somehow she was different now. Not once had he heard her whine or complain, even when he knew she must be exhausted. He scowled at the thought of the number of times he had felt guilty, his heart wrenched by her pale face and the black circles under her eyes, no matter how hard she tried to use makeup as camouflage.

He had to do something. He had to come up with a way to earn a living, a way to sort out his marriage, a way to tell Beth. . . .

There was a firm nudge at his arm again. Determinedly, Art again forced back the dark shadows that could so easily settle on him. "Okay, Bonnie, enough deep thinkin' for my first mornin' alone."

As he made for the gate in the fence again, he smiled

slightly at himself. Talking to the dog out loud could quickly become a habit.

The ramp leading to the front door was fairly steep, and when he reached the patio he was a little breathless. He vowed that the ramp they erected to replace the four steps from the back door into the yard would not be as steep, even if longer. He swung open the flyscreen door and then stared with dismay at the front door.

It must have slammed shut when he was in the backyard. No handle, just a lock. For a moment he could not believe what had happened. Then it hit him. He swore violently. "Locked out! You stupid idiot, you've let yourself be locked out!"

For one ghastly moment he had a vision of himself still sitting outside when Beth arrived home, especially if that hospital car never turned up. Even worse, what if Beth rang and he didn't answer the phone? Then all her doubts about leaving him by himself would be justified.

"No way," he said through gritted teeth. "She has enough to worry about."

He thought furiously. *Might be able to find a neighbor home.* Perhaps there would be a window open. Then he grinned. The kids had been playing with Bonnie in the back yard until Beth's exasperated shout had told them to hurry-up-and-get-in-the-car-or-else. Hopefully they had not turned the lock on the back door.

He took a frustrating, exhausting thirty minutes to find somebody at home in the neighborhood, or at least some-one who would answer his shouts from the bottom of their front steps. A furious German shepherd had made him beat a very hasty retreat from one yard.

The old man who eventually peered out at him proved, after a brief explanation, to be very friendly, overly helpful, and equally loquacious.

"Lucky it's only a little hilly round here," the old man puffed behind him. He had tucked his walking stick under one arm, grabbed the arms of the wheelchair despite Art's protests, and pushed him back to the house. "Youse woulda found the goin' pretty hard in that contraption. Had to use one for a while after I broke me hip. Now, you wait out here at the front while I try that back door."

Bonnie proved a stumbling block. Art heard her friendly, welcoming barks, and the old man reappeared, rapidly wielding his walking stick. Before he could open his mouth, Art roared, "Bonnie!"

There was silence. Art smiled. "She won't bite. Not much more than a puppy still."

Although still young, Bonnie was a full-sized, gorgeous example of a "Lassie dog," and Art could not really blame his helper for looking doubtful. But, after hesitating momentarily, he disappeared again. Art heard him talking soothing "dog talk" for a brief few moments, and then he relaxed as he heard the back screen door slam shut. A moment later, a triumphant old man was holding the front door open gallantly.

"Thank you, sir, very much," Art said fervently as he wheeled himself inside.

"Oh, me name's Ernie. Everyone calls me Ernie. Been living in this street for over sixty years. Came here when Edith and I married, ya know." He followed Art inside. "She's been gone these last ten years now, has my Edith. Still miss her. Now, what about I make you a nice cup of tea?"

Once again, Art's protests were overruled. But when he was at last sharing a hot cup of tea, he realized how exhausted he felt and was grateful for the drink, even though he wished he could rest quietly by himself.

He soon realized, though, how lonely the old man was. In fact, Ernie proved to have stories of the Second World War that fascinated Art. He told them with such fervor and dry humor that when he at last made moves to leave, Art was genuinely sorry to see him go.

When Art did eventually wave good-bye to his new friend, he felt very weary, and looked longingly at his bed. He had done the transfer from wheelchair to bed plenty of times in the hospital, but he still wasn't quite game enough to try it with no one about, mainly in case he could not get back on by himself. So he retreated to the lounge and made do by carefully lifting his legs up onto a stool. Then he was only too glad to sit quietly for a while.

The shrill ring of the phone woke him from a light doze. "How are you going, Art?" Beth's anxious voice asked.

His first instinct was not to tell her what had happened. She would only worry. So he said quickly, "I'm going very well, thank you, Mrs. Smith. How about your first morning?"

He could hear the relief in her voice as she replied, "No wonder they need my help in the morning! Just as well I started so early. I would have rung you sooner but the phone has hardly stopped ringing." Her tones softened. "Another customer has just come in. Must go."

Art replaced the phone receiver thoughtfully. Should he have told her? After all, he had coped quite well. He flexed his arms. His muscles would probably be a bit stiff later, and his hands were sore from pushing on the wheels. But he had coped! Jubilation swept through him.

When he unexpectedly heard the car and Beth's light, quick steps run up the ramp, he suddenly knew she had a right to know. She had been with him every step of the way so far. That fact made guilt sweep through him, but he pushed it aside and shrugged. "Just hope she doesn't become any more protective than she is already," he muttered as the front door swung open.

"This is an unexpected pleasure, Mrs. Smith." He forced a smile. "Got the sack already?"

"Nope. Bob came in and agreed to let me scoot home and have morning tea with my husband!"

Art stared at her. A memory of a young man tearing home for a brief morning tea time with his new young bride swept through him. They had been so in love then that they could not see enough of each other. Did she remember too?

Then his leaping pulse quieted. There was not a hint in her smiling face that she had come home on purpose so they could remember.

&

Not coming back to an empty house again was so good, Beth decided, and she found herself beaming at Art as he wheeled himself to meet her.

She studied his face carefully and his smile widened. He knew how concerned she had been having to leave him by himself. She made a rueful face at him. With considerable relief, she saw that he looked a little pale and tired, but otherwise great.

Just great.

A wave of love swept through her. She bent to brush her lips over his, wishing she was brave enough to kiss him properly, wishing he would grab her and kiss her. . .kiss her hard.

But he didn't. Disappointed, she moved away so he could not see her eyes, and said quickly, "We had such an early breakfast that I picked up some fish and chips for a snack."

She heard Art give a sigh of bliss. "You wonderful woman. I haven't had plain old fish and chips for ages and ages, especially wrapped in paper, and straight from take-away."

A pang shot through her. She should have remembered before this how much he loved the thick, salted hot potato chips and the deep fried, fish pieces in crisp batter.

"Well, I'll just get us a couple of plates and—"

"Nope."

She swung around in surprise. For a moment she was mesmerized by his flashing, laughing eyes.

"Don't need plates for a picnic." Before she could catch her breath, he reached for her hand and tugged. "Come on, let's have a picnic. I'm sure your boss won't want you to take too long, but there's a lovely sunny spot right in our own backyard." He hesitated, and his grin slipped a little. "You'd better push this contraption for me though."

Surprise flashed through her. He usually guarded his independence fiercely, and she had learned the hard way not to push his chair around.

He was watching her. "I'll tell you why in a moment." Before she could speak, he reached up and grabbed the bundle of food wrapped in several layers of white butcher paper. "Come on, before these get cold, or the car arrives for me."

They relaxed in the sun, Beth on a hastily grabbed blanket; the chips were still hot, and absolutely delicious.

"Hmm, I didn't realize how hungry I was." Beth reached for a piece of fish. "Now, tell me why you wanted me to push your chair out here."

Art hesitated, and then held his hands out. "That's why," he said very quietly.

"Blisters! Art, what on earth. . . ?"

"Now, now, don't go into a flat spin."

She relaxed slightly when Art gave a chuckle. He gestured toward the dog. "Blame Bonnie. It was her pitiful, don't-leave-me-kids barking that made me come around here to the backyard in the first place. Straight after you left this morning."

Beth tensed. Once she would have flown in with questions, words. She controlled her tongue with difficulty, and waited.

"The front door slammed shut and locked me out."

A puzzled look crossed Beth's face, and then she gasped in understanding. "Art, whatever did you do?"

"Well, first of all I believe I swore," he said thoughtfully. Then he looked up at her and grinned at her resigned expression. Quickly he told her what had happened, describing his new friend, Ernie, in graphic detail.

When he told her about Bonnie scaring Ernie, she looked down at the now blissfully sleeping dog stretched out on a corner of the rug. Suddenly her lips twitched. "He was scared of this ferocious animal?"

Art looked down at Bonnie. "I'll have you know Ernie was a hero of the armed forces *par excellence*! He was afraid of no enemy soldier or situation with his commanding officer. Especially when they caught him running an illegal gambling ring among his fellow soldiers," he added reflectively. "He took great pains for nearly an hour to make sure I appreciated that major fact."

His voice was indignant, but when he looked up his eyes were dancing. The laugh Beth had been trying to stifle spilled out. And then Art's hearty roar joined her.

When they eventually stopped laughing, Beth scrubbed at the tears running down her face. "I don't know why laughing so much always makes these stupid tears flow. And the last thing I should be doing is laughing, when you were locked out!"

Art was silent. When she looked up at him, his tender smile

made her catch her breath.

"I wouldn't have you any other way," he murmured. Their eyes suddenly clung. "It's good to see you shed laugh tears instead of the other kind for a change, Beth."

She was silent for a long moment, the laughter disappearing from her face. "It's good to have someone to laugh and cry with again."

Art looked down. He was silent for a long moment. "When we were first married I used to enjoy doing everything together with you, Beth. Well, that is, all except those times you tried to drag me to church. But then. . . ," he took a deep breath, ". . .then I didn't enjoy anything for a long time."

Beth was silent. Slowly she rolled up the remains of their fish and chips. At last she looked up at him. "I have to take the blame for that, Art. I've been wanting to apologize for the rotten nagging you had to endure, especially after Robbie was born. And I. . .I want you to promise me something."

He looked at her, surprised. Then he scowled.

She continued rapidly, "I want you to promise to put me over your knee and wallop me if I ever start up again."

Art's scowl deepened. Hurt lashed him. He had come so close to hitting her more than once. Then that last dreadful night. . . . He had been so frightened that he could sink to such depths; that had been the main reason he had left.

He fought for words. Fought to say how sorry he had immediately been, how bitterly ashamed he still was. But in all these months he had never found the words to tell her how he felt, and he couldn't now.

Then, as he stared at her, awareness hit him. She actually reckoned she had deserved his treatment of her! Sure, her hysterical nagging would have upset a saint, and he sure had been a long way from that, especially that last evening.

But he had always believed that no woman ever deserved being hit by any man worth anything, no matter the provocation.

He saw the haunted look of remembrance in her eyes. They also held something else, something he wasn't sure he was really seeing.

They stared at each other silently. Then suddenly, to his utter astonishment, he realized that her deep blue eyes were actually pleading for *his* forgiveness!

seven

Beth held her breath. She was scared.

Dare she put it any plainer? Would he reject her fumbling attempts to let him know she realized now how much she had provoked him that last night, how much she had been to blame for so much that had gone wrong in their marriage?

He had really frightened her, though, that last dreadful fight the night before he had walked out.

Jacky had been sick, very sick. By the time Art should have been home, her vomiting and diarrhea had left her so listless and pale Beth had known she had to get the small girl to a doctor. Her purse had been practically empty, ruling out a taxi.

The last few months Art had been staying later and later at the pub where he met his mates after work. And that night he had been later than ever before. By the time he had deigned to come home she had been frantic with fear and worry.

As soon as she had heard his key in the door she had flown at him, smelt the alcohol on him, and screamed that he cared more for his mates than her. That his daughter had needed him, but what did he care?

There had been more, much more. He had yelled back at her, even cursed her, and then, "You're nothing but a nagging, useless nuisance."

Then his fist had lashed out at her. She had managed to dodge the blow, but she had tripped and fallen. Her face had hit the kitchen bench and the pain made her cry out. A trickle of blood had run down her cheek. It was only a tiny cut, but the bruise had been there for days.

Dazed and frightened, she had stared up at him from the floor. Never would she forget the look on his face as he stared down at her. He reached out his hand and started to bend down toward her. She had cringed away, scared he would try and hit her again.

Every drop of color had drained from Art's face. Horror had stared from his eyes. He had reeled back as though he'd been struck himself. His expression had changed again. The tears streaming down her face had blurred her vision. Many times she had tried to work out what his expression should have told her. Had it been guilt, hopelessness, anguish, or all three?

Still crouched on the floor, she had tried to stifle the sob that burst from her, wiping at the tears to clear her vision, smearing her face with blood. Then Art had slammed some money down onto the kitchen bench and walked out. His look of fury and disgust had haunted her ever since. How could a man still love someone who disgusted him as much as she had?

Now, as she stared at Art, waiting tensely for his reaction, she wondered if this could be a chance to at last put it all into words. At first, he had been so ill in hospital that she had been just content to be there with him, sometimes even daring to hold his hand.

When he had recovered from the worst of the burns, and been still undergoing tests to find out the extent of his spinal injury, she had tried to find the right time to talk about their marriage. But despite his accusation after Gail and Jim's wedding, that she was the one who refused to talk about it, he had told her in those earlier days that there was no point raking up the past while his future was so uncertain. Since then though, she had been the reluctant one, scared that he wanted to leave them again.

Only once had she made any attempt to talk to him about the night he had left. Such a dreadful look of pain and anguish had entered his eyes before he had turned quickly away that she had been deeply shocked. He had muttered a stifled "Don't, please," and not spoken for the rest of her visit. At the time, the doctors in Sydney had already been worried about his continuing depression. She had been so frightened she would only make things worse, so she had not said another word.

"Art," she began fearfully, "I mean it. I've always been so very sorry for my behavior that night. I didn't know. . ." She swallowed, and continued a little steadier, "I'm so sorry that after you lost your job you found it easier to stay at the pub with your friends than come home."

Art was still scowling, and Beth's heart dropped.

"When you didn't come home. . .days after you disappeared that night, one of your mates told me how they'd been trying to cheer you up, offering suggestions of job prospects available despite the rural recession."

She hesitated again, and when he still did not look at her she said slowly, "I went for counselling to Rance Telford, you know."

Art lifted his head and stared up at her with an arrested look in his eyes.

"It. . .it took me a long time to acknowledge my own failures in our marriage. For a long time there was very little reason for you to want to come home to—just a nagging, selfish wife, undisciplined children, and an unkempt house," she said sadly.

Rance Telford had proven to be a wise Christian counsellor. As well as helping her sort through specific issues, he had above all pointed her to God's Word and what it had to say about husband and wife relationships, about winning your unbelieving husband by your behavior. She had studied, prayed, and cried many tears of repentance for her initial disobedience and then her part in the breakdown of their marriage.

Beth took a deep breath. "I can't blame you for putting off as long as you could coming home that night to me and the children."

She had also often wondered if he had been afraid to tell her there would be no definite pay packet the next week, if that had been why he had blustered and roared back at her as she had flung all those dreadful accusations at him.

The first couple of days afterward she had been very busy with the ill Jacky, but then she had become more and more frightened when he had not come home. She had phoned a few of his friends, found out about his losing his job. When a week had dragged by with not a word from him, she had been frantic.

By the next weekend she had not been able to stand the uncertainty and the dreadful sense of being alone. She had packed up the kids and visited her mother and Jim, pouring out her heart to them for advice and help. They had been loving and supportive. Jim especially had been very concerned for his friend, but he had sadly reminded her that by marrying someone who wasn't a Christian she had disobeyed God's ways to start with. Her mother was the one who had suggested she needed counselling herself.

When she had returned home, Art had been there and gone. He had taken all his clothes and left a brief note.

She could not believe that the young man she had married with such love could have left her with only a note that simply said "I've been retrenched, but now I've the chance of a job interstate. I'll put money in our joint account when I can, but please don't try to contact me. You and the kids are better off without me. I can't stand any more."

She had felt as though a vital part of her had been ripped out. Never would she have believed she could hurt so much. She had called out desperately to God for help, and she had wondered many times since how she would have survived those dark days without Jesus.

Each fortnight the money had been deposited in their joint account. Sometimes there had only been small amounts, and she had worried about how he was managing himself, if he was on unemployment benefits. Then the weeks had stretched to six months, with no other contact. She'd had to face up to the bitter fact he never intended coming back to her and the children.

She knew she had changed a lot in those months after his disappearance. Then, one fortnight, no money was put into the bank. Her only contact with Art had ceased.

And she had known. Even before the grave-faced policeman had knocked on her door, she had known something terrible had happened to the only man she would ever love.

"I'm so sorry, Art," she whispered.

As she stared at him pleadingly, to Beth's immense relief, slowly, ever so slowly, his lips smiled. Then her relief dimmed. The smile did not reach Art's hazel eyes. They were filled with sadness.

"You're pretty safe," he drawled. "Ernie would take great exception to his new friend man-handling his pretty wife!"

For a moment she was bewildered. Then she remembered what she had said about giving him permission to wallop her. Her answering smile was a little tremulous. Not even for a moment would she let him see how disappointed she was that he had chosen not to respond to anything else she had said.

She tilted her chin. "I guess I'll be quite safe then."

His eyes darkened even further. The smile was gone in a flash. "You'll always be safe with me, Beth. Always."

The words were a sincere promise. A vow.

She was a little puzzled. Of course she was safe with Art. Except for that one lapse he had always been so protective.

For a moment longer she stared at him, wondering if she should force him to talk about it all. Should she dare to at last put it all into words? She had to try to convince him how sorry she was for her part in the disintegration of their marriage, that she knew now how she had carried on like a spoiled, immature brat instead of a woman who professed faith in a loving and giving God.

Would he understand how afraid she was he would never forgive her, that their relationship could never be completely healed? Did he have any idea how desperately unhappy she was because she feared he no longer loved her enough to really want to come home and be together as a family again?

As it had so many times before, fear of saying the wrong thing, of not being able to convince him how she felt, stopped her. She was terrified if she brought it out into the open anymore, he would be forced to put his feelings into words. Be forced to tell her. . .tell her he didn't love her anymore.

Beth slowly scrambled to her feet. Hating herself for her cowardice, she managed to say brightly "Well, you won't be ready for your physio appointment if we don't break up this picnic, and Bob will think I've got lost."

She stopped, and then in a desperate attempt to cancel out other words she longed to be able to say, she blurted out, "Art, do you think these extra sessions at the hospital will really improve the muscle tone of your legs, stop them getting any thinner?"

She dared to give him a quick, darting look as she moved away. The expression on Art's face made her pause. Then he saw her looking at him, and his expression went blank.

Again.

Beth frowned inwardly. Had she been wrong? Had he been about to talk about their separation, their marriage? For one brief moment she thought she had seen disappointment, even hurt. Then there had been another expression, almost like fear.

But now, as had happened so many times before, Art deliberately chose not to let her know what he was thinking. He grinned a little crookedly. "So the powers that be reckon. Guess we'll just have to wait and see." Averting his face, he started his chair forward, adding quickly, "Come on, can't miss out on the torture session, can we? Especially since they went to so much trouble to work the available transport and appointments out for us."

Beth agreed as calmly as she could, hoping he could not see the way her hands were trembling. Quickly taking her position behind him, she started the wheelchair up the path. Fear kept its clutch on her heart. She knew that one day soon they would have to talk about their marriage and future together.

Oh, Father, I so need Your strength here, she prayed silently, *but I'm just plain scared.*

Terrified *might be the correct word*, she thought grimly, terrified she would say the wrong thing as she had so many times before, do the wrong thing that would put the last nail in the coffin of their marriage.

When he was still in the hospital, she had been able to convince herself they had plenty of time to sort out their marriage. But now he was home; she knew they would not be able to put the subject off indefinitely.

Despite her apprehension, during the days that followed, Art never once mentioned their relationship again. His leg muscles seemed to be responding to the treatment. At least, she could see they were not still getting thinner as they had been before. If anything, at times she thought they were actually getting more and more back to normal. She knew that could not be with paralyzed legs, that it must be more her own wishful thinking that made her think so. However, he gradually became increasingly independent, managing most things for himself from his chair.

The days began to fly by for Beth. Janet's baby arrived early, and Beth's hours varied considerably, depending on the workload and when Bob could be in the office. The extra money was a relief, but she became very tired. She knew Art fretted about her working hard, so she tried her best not to let him see how exhausted she was some days.

She was thrilled at how much he helped around the house. Sometimes she was astounded at what he managed to accomplish while she was at work. Beds were made, dishes cleared away, and clothes neatly ironed. One day he triumphantly told her he had washed the kitchen and bathroom floors; he looked immensely pleased at her heartfelt thanks.

Before, he had never helped her very much at all, and she had accepted that because he had worked very long hours himself. But she had often thought, especially after the babies had arrived, that he could have helped a bit more.

Some days, Beth even found herself becoming concerned at how much he did do for her. Occasionally his physio sessions really exhausted him. After the first few times, she had given up asking him about them because he had been very terse, not wanting to "rehash the torture" as he put it.

Beth had paid a very rushed visit to see Janet and her baby while they had still been in the hospital. Each day the proud new father regaled her with progress reports, but one quiet Saturday morning she asked Art if he minded keeping an eye on the kids while she paid them a visit.

He smiled approvingly at her. "No problem. I think the plan is to teach Bonnie some new tricks this morning anyway."

An answering smile lit up her face. "I hope I know the first one you'll teach her," she teased him.

"Of course," he said haughtily with a raised eyebrow. "Not to dig up your new pansy plants will be the very first on the list."

Beth laughed ruefully. "Seeing half of them have already been replanted twice, I don't think you'll have much success there. Actually, I was hoping it might be that she learns she's supposed to sleep in her own kennel outside and not sneak into certain males' bedrooms inside this establishment!"

Art managed to look suitably sheepish for a moment. "Well," he drawled, "apparently she decided the carpet in my room was more comfortable than the one in Robbie's. Besides," he added reasonably, "it was raining outside and pretty cold."

Beth threw up her hands. "All the more reason to keep a wet, smelly dog dripping mud everywhere outside!"

"Well, it wasn't this male who let him in."

Her eyes softened. "But this male was too soft-hearted to get the other male to chase him out."

Beth thought about the yearning look that flashed into her husband's face all the way to the Lane's house. She knew he was trying so hard to get Robbie to accept him, relax around him, and she had not for one serious moment minded a bit of mud and a few more dog's hairs, if there was any chance father and son could enjoy each other's company as they once had.

Janet and Bob were outside in the front garden when she pulled up. Janet was sitting quietly in a deck chair while Bob was industriously using a digging fork.

"Don't get up," Beth protested as Janet greeted her with a smile and stood up.

Janet stretched. "Almost time for the baby's next feed, and I need a cuppa first."

Bob grinned at them, sweat running down his cheerful face. "You girls go ahead and have your drinks so you can goo-gaa at the baby when he wakes. If I stop now, I'll never get up the energy again to finish this garden bed."

They laughed and left him to it. As Janet bustled around preparing a pot of tea, they chatted about the business and babies. It wasn't until they were both nibbling on some chocolate cookies and sipping their hot drinks that Janet asked how Art was going.

Beth put down her cup carefully. "Very well," she said automatically as she usually did when anyone enquired. Then she stopped and looked up at Janet. "As. . .as far as I know, he's doing well," she added suddenly.

"As far as you know?"

Beth hesitated. "There's just something. . .Oh, I'm just being silly," she burst out suddenly, "but he never has wanted to talk to me about his condition at all. He never has since the accident, but now. . ."

Janet waited silently, and Beth found herself telling her about the times she had thought Art was concealing something from her. "When he was in the hospital I could always ask the nurses as well as his doctor. The other day I even rang his doctor from your office." She shrugged. "He seemed rather surprised that I had rung, but he said Art was doing very well. So I suppose I'm just imagining there's something wrong. It's just a feeling I have, I suppose. But he's so tired some nights after his sessions at the hospital. Sometimes he seems to have quite a lot more pain too, although he usually refuses to take any painkillers stronger than paracetamol. Says he must have been close to being a drug addict in the hospital."

The healthy bellow of a tiny baby sounded from the bedroom. Janet hesitated and then stood up. "Would you like to come and talk to me while I feed him?"

Beth stood up too. "No, no," she said quickly, "I didn't intend to be away too long, but I would love a peep at him."

Janet beamed, and led the way into the small bedroom that had been converted into an attractive nursery. Beth willingly agreed Robert Junior was truly gorgeous. But she had to say a rather hurried farewell as the demand for food became more and more urgent.

Janet carried the squawking infant to the door to see Beth out. Rocking the baby in an effort to soothe him she said quickly, "Before you go, I must ask you. Is there any chance we'll see you at church tomorrow?"

"I'm not sure," Beth said wistfully. "I certainly have been missing fellowship and worship."

On the way home, she thought carefully about how she could broach the subject to Art. There was no way she wanted her church attendance to cause any strife between her and her husband again. She had spent a lot of time in prayer about it all, and she knew she had put off long enough mentioning it to Art. She sent another fervent prayer about it heavenward.

To her utter astonishment, that night after the children

were in bed and she had rejoined him in front of the television, he said very casually, "You haven't been to church since we moved to Brisbane, Beth. Haven't you found a church to go to yet?"

She gaped at him, and then looked quickly back at the television when he glanced at her.

"Well, er, yes. As a matter of fact Janet wants me to go with them tomorrow morning," she said rapidly. Then she hesitated before adding softly, "I went to church too many years without you Art, and I. . .I. . .I don't want going to church to be an issue between us ever again." She couldn't continue and fidgeted with her skirt, avoiding his eyes.

"Do they have a Sunday school for the kids?"

His voice was abrupt, and her eyes flew to his face. She could tell nothing from his expression.

She took a deep breath. "Yes, I believe they do. It's called junior church and it's during part of the worship service, after the communion time."

"Good."

She stared at him, but his expression was hidden. "Art. . . you. . .you don't mind if we go to church tomorrow?"

There was genuine astonishment on the face he turned to her. "Mind? Why on earth should I mind?"

"Because. . .because. . ." Beth stopped helplessly.

The expression on Art's face changed. "Because I refused to go with you, never meant I minded you going, Beth!"

"You didn't? But I. . .I thought. . ."

Her voice died away and she stared back at him, remembering all the times they had argued about Christian issues. So many times they had even ended up in furious, shouting arguments about such things as whether there really was a God who cared a scrap about what happened to ordinary people, about whether you had to read your Bible every day and go to church to be a Christian.

"Beth, I wanted you to do whatever you felt you should." His eyes looked away, and she saw him swallow. "It just. . . your going off to church without me made me feel pretty dreadful sometimes. As though you were all good, and I was all bad." The words burst quickly from him.

She gave a startled disclaimer, and he shrugged. Still avoiding her eyes, he added softly, "I know thinking that was pretty stupid. No person is all bad and no person all good, but it *was* the way I felt. That's why I always tried to make sure I arranged to do things on Sundays so I wouldn't be left in an empty house."

Beth felt her eyes fill with tears. There had been numerous Sundays when he must have felt lonely, neglected. If she had been less full of herself, less inflexible and not blind to his own needs, she could have gone with him sometimes. No wonder they had drifted apart those years after Robbie had arrived.

"I'm so sorry, Art, dear. I never realized. . ." Her voice wobbled, but she controlled it with an effort. "It doesn't matter about going to church, Art, I'll. . ."

"Beth, did I ever, even once, ask you not to go to church?"

"No," she said very thoughtfully after a long pause, "no, you never actually asked me not to go, but I knew you resented the fact that I went. And I can't really blame you. My attitude was very bad."

He looked uncomfortable. "I resented those wounded, sometimes angry looks I got because I refused to go with you."

"I did more than look, I'm afraid," muttered Beth remorsefully.

"Yeah, you sure did have a good turn of phrase on occasion," he drawled.

Beth sat up straight. "Art, I'm never going to pest you about going to church ever again."

Art returned her anxious look for a long moment. A rather strange expression crossed his own face. "Ever again, huh?"

"I. . .I've already said how sorry I am for the way I behaved about that, Art," Beth said, fighting back a sudden desire to weep.

"So, if I ever have a sudden urge to go to church I have to ask you to take me, do I?"

Beth caught her breath in sudden hope. She bit her tongue and gave a brief nod. Then her hope died when he turned his head away and suddenly swung his wheelchair around and started it rolling toward the door.

"Good," he spat out as though he was angry, "very good. I'm going to bed. You'd better help me up before you leave in the morning. Oh," he stopped and glanced at her briefly, "Robbie and Jacky will want to go to Sunday school or whatever they call it. While you were out they told me they missed going. Apparently they blamed me for that too. Couldn't understand why you hadn't taken them."

He had disappeared from the room before Beth had gathered her scattered wits enough to reply.

eight

Art spent a more restless night than he had for a long time. He tried to convince himself it was because he had not had a chance to do the exercises in his room.

He had not done the exercises because Beth had followed him to his room, quietly helped him as she always had to, but then, when he had been at last tucked into bed, bent, kissed him full on his lips, and whispered, "Thank you, Art." He'd felt guilty and an absolute heel.

She'd actually thanked him for telling her he did not mind if she went to church! And then, he'd actually felt disappointed, even angry because she wasn't going to ask him to go with her! There was so much she didn't know, so much to tell her, and he didn't know how to start.

Desperately he tried to push away the memories their conversation had stirred up. He had been haunted for so long by Beth's terrified figure cringing away from him on the floor.

The next time he had seen her had been through a haze of painkillers. For one weak moment, he had been so pleased to see her again, even though her face had been pale with shock and fear.

Now he was tormented by the fear he had done the wrong thing, letting her stay with him all those months. But her presence had been the only thing he'd had to cling to through the horror. Certainly he had made a few weak attempts to persuade her to go home to the children, especially when they'd had chicken pox, but when she had finally gone for a couple of weeks. . . .

He shuddered.

Sometime in the darkest hour of the night, he acknowledged once and for all how much Beth had changed. He wasn't sure he even liked all of that change. Sure, she no longer nagged him and tried to boss him around like she used to. She was also far more tolerant. She was much gentler, more considerate. She handled the children superbly. Come to that, she handled him superbly too!

But she was so subdued, so much quieter than the exuberant, glowing young girl he had married. He could only remember twice in recent months when she had shown in any way that the old spirited Beth was still around. Once had been that day he had "carried" her over the threshold. The other time. . .the other time had been when her indomitable spirit had leapt out at him as she had vehemently declared they would cope.

Then he remembered what else she had said that day. They would cope with God's strength. He still wasn't too sure God would be bothered with himself, but He surely must be helping a lovely woman like Beth.

At last he fell into a restless sleep, but he was feeling decidedly out of sorts when an excited young voice woke him at the same time that a small hand shook his arm.

"Daddy, come on, you've got to wake up 'cause we're goin' to church!"

He groaned, and then opened his eyes. The hand on his arm was snatched away. Robbie was staring at him. An anxious expression suddenly killed the excited, flushed look on his little face. He took a step away from the bed.

"Do your legs hurt, Daddy?" his small voice asked. "Won't you be able to come with us?"

"Robbie!" an exasperated voice exclaimed from the

doorway. "Why are you waking your father up so early?"

Robbie looked across at his mother and then back at Art. "You. . .you said we had to hurry up and have breakfast so we could go to church. But Daddy just groaned, so I s'pose he can't come."

His face dropped even further with obvious disappointment, and Art's heart suddenly went out to his small son. He looked across at Beth. She looked distressed and opened her mouth, but to his own surprise he heard himself say, "Oh, that was only a moan because I had to wake up early to get ready for church. I'm certainly not in pain anywhere."

Beth's eyes rounded with astonishment, and then her face lit up as though a light had been turned on deep inside her. Something inside Art splintered into little pieces. She actually wanted him with them that much!

Beth opened her mouth again, and then closed it. He saw her swallow, and he wasn't sure which touched him most, her obvious delight, or the way Robbie's eyes began to dance.

"That's great, Daddy!"

Art's voice sounded rough to his own ears as he growled, "Go on you two. What are you hanging around for? What time do we have to be ready to leave?"

"Mummy said we had exactly one hour to get ready," Jacky's cross voice said from behind Beth. "And I've just fed Bonnie, but nobody's got *my* breakfast yet!"

Beth still seemed to being having difficulty finding her voice, so he growled again, "Because you're old enough to get your own. Go on you two kids, hop to it!"

When they were alone, Art kept his face averted and said shortly, "I'll skip my shower today. If you bring me a dish of water and chuck me some clean clothes, I shouldn't take long."

"Art, are you sure. . . ?"

He cut fiercely across Beth's ragged voice with, "It's the first time in a very long while that my son actually looked disappointed at the thought I couldn't go somewhere with him. I don't care where we're going. I'm going because he wants me with him."

He almost added, "And you obviously still do too," but instead he looked up at Beth defiantly. Immediately he wished he had said the words, for a sad look crossed her face before she turned away.

He felt suddenly full of guilt. For the first time he realized just how bitterly disappointed she must have been when he had not wanted to go to church with her. And now he had just stated he did not want to disappoint Robbie, but he hadn't said anything about not wanting to disappoint *her*.

He opened his mouth to say something. . .anything, as long as it took her sadness away, but she was already at the door with a murmur about fetching some water, and the moment was gone.

❧

Beth hurriedly grabbed a basin, held it under the tap, and turned on the water. Suddenly she closed her eyes. Art was actually going to church with her!

"Thank You, Lord!"

She had not realized she had spoken out loud until Robbie's voice said loudly, "Stop talking to Jesus and hurry up, Mum. I don't want to be late for Sunday school."

With a stifled laugh, Beth fled. "Like father, like son," she thought as she raced to be ready in time.

❧

The suburban church was large, and the car park was almost full by the time the Smiths arrived. Several people murmured friendly greetings, but Art heard a relieved note in Beth's voice when she was hailed by a young couple carrying a baby basket.

As always, Art had steeled himself for the curious looks he usually received, but as Beth quickly introduced Bob and Janet Lane, he saw nothing but enthusiasm in their two beaming faces.

"It's good to meet you at last, Art. We've heard so much about you," Bob said with a smile and a firm handshake.

Art threw a glance at Beth. She flushed a little self-consciously but tilted her chin.

Before he could speak, she said hurriedly, "We'd better hurry, it's almost starting time," leaving him to eye her thoughtfully, wondering just what she had said about him to make her blush.

❧

The church service came very close to being a disaster from start to finish. First of all there the church had no ramp and they had difficulty getting the chair up the long steps of the beautiful old building. Fortunately, Bob was there to help, but Beth knew how much Art must be hating the added attention.

Then the church had only old-fashioned pews so that Art had to sit in the aisle, a few rows from the entrance. By his scowl every now and again, Gail knew how conspicuous he was feeling.

To make it worse, the well-meaning minister welcomed him so profusely that Beth squirmed in sympathy for him. Then she was really furious when the insensitive dolt fervently prayed for "our dear brother in the wheelchair." She opened her eyes and looked frantically across at Art just in time to meet his eyes.

Her own widened. He was grinning madly. Then he winked at her, and actually dared to shake his finger at her in admonition for not having her eyes closed during the prayer time. She felt hot color flood her face, and she hurriedly shut her eyes again.

≈

Art's eyes lingered on her for the rest of the prayer. She was more beautiful than ever today. Certainly she looked very different from the last time he'd been in church with her at Jim and Gail's wedding, but she was a delight to behold in her simple, fresh cotton dress.

He had known she would be upset by the minister mentioning him specifically. Glancing up at her in time to catch her worried look had been instinctive. In fact, to his own surprise he had not really minded being mentioned as much as he probably would have. The prayer was so sincere, so earnest. Besides, he needed every prayer available!

Certainly, the way the service had started, Art had expected to feel out of place and uncomfortable. Beth had been pretty embarrassed about having to accept Bob Lane's help, but he had been relieved to be able to "park" near the back of the church where he did not have to endure everyone's eyes.

Even that rather too exuberant welcome had not bothered him too much. At least the guy was not pretending the wheelchair did not exist as so many people did when confronted with it the first time.

He was still staring at Beth when the "amen" was said and she looked up straight at him again. This time she smiled gently with such tenderness in her expression that he turned hurriedly away.

Suddenly he wondered if she prayed for him. And he knew the answer immediately. Of course she did. No doubt she always had. When they had first been married she had tried and tried to get him to read the Bible and pray together with her after the evening meal. If she had but known, he'd inwardly recoiled in horror. Some of his worst memories of his father had been when he had insisted they have "family devotions." It had been anything but "family" and far from "devotion."

A rousing time of song interrupted his thoughts. It was led by an enthusiastic young song leader with an electric guitar. He was helped by an accomplished pianist, a girl playing clarinet, and a gray-haired man on a violin. There was even a drummer behind a small set of drums. An overhead projector threw up the words of each song on a large white screen above the platform.

Art was surprised, and sat up a little straighter. His father's ultra-conservative hair would have stood straight up at this setup!

Art did not know most of the songs, but everyone else seemed to be enjoying singing them with gusto. He glanced at Jacky and Robbie. They were watching everything with wide eyes.

Beth turned her head and caught his eye. He grinned at her again, and she gave him a rather relieved smile back. Then she turned back to sing the words of the current song.

Art found the melody haunting, and a reverent stillness had come over the people as they sang about longing after God as a deer pants for water. Art did not know how a deer felt when it was thirsty, but there had been many times in those days in the hospital burn unit that his tongue and mouth had been very dry, especially after surgery and skin grafts. He didn't think he had ever thirsted for God anything like that, though.

Before he really had time to dwell on it all, they started singing very quietly a song he knew only too well. He had learned it as a boy when he had been forced to go to nearly every meeting at his parents' church. All around him heads were lowered in prayer as they sang softly and reverently. But Art kept his head erect, staring up at the words.

How could the things of earth—like a rotten home life, a broken marriage, a horrible accident, a broken body—possibly become "strangely dim" just by looking into the face of Jesus!

Then they sang the chorus again. Art looked around. Even Robbie knew it and was singing quietly, his feet swinging to and fro. Jacky was sneaking a look at two girls her own age in the seat behind. He saw Beth touch her gently, and she obediently faced the front again.

Then he focused on Beth. As he watched her, she closed her eyes again. Once again, he feasted his eyes on her through the prayer that followed. He saw her nod a couple of times, her lips moving in a silent "amen." Then she gently wiped at her eyes, and he looked quickly away, feeling like an intruder into her deepest feelings about God. To see Beth moved to tears in such a way affected him so deeply he had not a clue what was being said by the song leader as he prayed.

Despite all the problems that her religion had caused in the latter part of their marriage, he had never doubted Beth's belief in God. At times the extent of her commitment to her church had so scared him it had made him angry. At times he had even blamed that commitment for harming their husband-wife relationship, had even, in his most honest moments, acknowledged a tinge of jealousy that she had never seemed as committed to him. And yet he had never had any doubt that she loved him, plain, ordinary Art Smith, at least not until after Robbie was born.

Suddenly, for the first time ever, he wanted to believe like Beth. He wanted so much to believe in a God who really cared. Fear that belief would demand commitment swept over him. He clenched his jaw. This was crazy thinking. Look at how commitment to their church had made his father and mother behave.

But Gail's commitment had not made her like them.

His hands clenched on the hymnbook he had been handed as they entered. Suddenly, for the first time, he saw very clearly the vast difference between his parents' fanatical commitment to their church and Beth's commitment to her God. He realized how stupid he'd been.

His parents' commitment had made them obey every narrow dictate their church imposed on its members. Their commitment to their church had made them rule their only child with a rod of iron.

Beth's commitment was to a loving Heavenly Father, entirely different from the God of anger and retribution he had been taught to fear.

Sure, when they'd first started going out together, he had sneered silently at Beth's attempts to remain pure, holy. "Keeping herself for marriage" had been the way she had put it. The bitter teenager he had been had equated that with the religious rules and regulations his parents had insisted he keep, and against which he had rebelled. At long last he had managed to persuade her differently. But he had always felt a trace of shame that he had only succeeded in seducing her when she had been so upset by her father's death. It had only happened the once. He had seen how stricken with guilt she had been, even more so when they found out she was pregnant.

Over the years, especially as their marriage had deteriorated, one thought had haunted him. Would she ever have married him if that night of loving had never taken place first?

These past months had made him see that her deeper commitment to Christ made her more loving, gave her strength to put up with an unlovable husband. But how *could* God love a man like him? He doubted very much that even the type of God that Beth believed in would accept such a man as he.

❧

Beth saw Art's clenched hands and her eyes flew to his face. It was so grim, her heart plunged. She had been thrilled that after so many years, Art was sitting beside her in church again. But if he hated it. . . .

"Oh, Lord. . . ," she breathed silently, ". . .please may Your Spirit open his eyes and his heart to Your love. Make Jesus real to him."

Beth had never found out for sure just why Art had become so antagonistic to going to church. She believed it had a lot to do with his parents, but she had never been able to get him to talk much about them. He had really surprised her last night when he had said he had never minded her going, just her insistence that he go also. She still doubted that statement of his. He *had* resented her going, she was sure of it.

When she had wanted to be involved in mid-week activities he had been even more resistant, several times informing her sharply not to take for granted that he was her built-in baby-sitter.

She shifted nervously in her seat. Sometimes she had yelled back at him and gone anyway. She tugged at her lower lip with her top teeth.

Rance had pointed her to the scriptures that had told her how displeasing that type of attitude was to God. Through studying the scriptures and prayer, she was still becoming more aware of God's mind on such behavior.

With a start she realized Art had whispered something to her. She looked at him, and he nodded toward Robbie's anxious face.

"Mum," Robbie whispered loudly, "can we go too now?"

Beth glanced around and then felt her face go hot. While she had been deep in memories, some announcement had been made about the children leaving for their junior church.

"They're to go out while we're singing the second verse," Art murmured.

She nodded briefly at Robbie, and avoided his father's amused eyes. Self-consciously she found the number in her own hymnbook as Art pointed to his.

"Mum!"

Beth glanced down at Robbie. He was looking up at her with a scared look on his face. Then he shrank against her and watched the other children moving down the aisle toward the entrance.

She hesitated briefly and then whispered, "You don't have to go out if you don't want to."

She felt Art move suddenly, and she looked down at him. He had a most peculiar look on his face as he watched them.

A small voice whispered loudly, "I want to go, but. . ."

"Would you like me to come with you this first time so you know where to go?"

Jacky was already disappearing with the little girl who had been sitting behind them. A little hand slipped into Beth's. She rolled her eyes at Art and led Robbie out. In a few moments they spotted Bob Lane coming toward them.

"Let me show you where to go, young man," he said softly. He winked at Beth, and with relief she felt Robbie's clinging hand let go and without another look at her he went with Bob.

Art was watching for her return. He gave a relieved smile as she joined him. "Everything okay?" he murmured.

She nodded, joined in singing the last of the hymn, and

sat down with considerable relief to enjoy the rest of the service. A large hand reached across and closed on hers. She turned sharply. Art's eyes were soft. Love whelmed up in her for him and she folded her fingers tightly around his. Their eyes clung for a moment, and then Art looked away.

The tenseness had gone from his jaw, and every sense in Beth rose up in thankfulness that he was sitting here beside her, certainly not "all in one piece" but alive and not gone from her forever. And so they sat hand in hand until the end of the service.

Only Jacky chattered excitedly on the way home in the car. Beth glanced several times at Robbie's set expression. She saw that Art had also noticed that something had seriously upset the small boy.

"Well, Robbie, and how did you enjoy your class? Did you make any new friends?" Art caught Beth's concerned eyes as he spoke, and then turned slightly so he could see Robbie's face.

"They were all dumb!" There was a distinct waver in the angry words.

"You're the dumb one," Jacky said haughtily. "My new friend said her brother in your class thought you didn't know nothin'."

Before Art or Beth could speak, Robbie let out a stifled sob, then turned on his sister and shouted, "Well, I'd never heard that dumb old story about that dumb man being let down through that dumb roof before."

"He wasn't dumb, stupid, he was paralyzed like Dad."

Beth and Art looked at each other. Beth opened her mouth in dismay, but Art shook his head slightly at her.

"That's enough, you two." Art's voice was stern. "We've just left church and you shouldn't be speaking to each other like that. Not another word until we get home!"

"That's what Mum always says," grumbled Jacky.

"Jacky, not another word!"

Art had raised his voice, but he managed to control his twitching lips, even when Beth shot a gleam of sheer amusement at him.

She refrained from saying anything until the car was parked in the driveway. "I said exactly the same thing to them their first day back at school after Easter," she murmured for his ears only as she placed his chair next to the car. "In fact," she added thoughtfully, "something had upset Robbie then, and I never did find out what had happened."

"Well, I think that this time we should," Art said quietly.

Both children had bolted for the backyard. Their parents' eyes followed them, and then Beth sighed. "Oh, well, guess I'd better go and see what's upset Robbie. It's a shame. He was so pleased about going."

"Beth. . ." Art paused, searching her face as she turned to him. "I think perhaps I should sort this out."

A shadow touched Beth's eyes. "Art—" she burst out, and then bit her lip, her face uncertain.

"I know, love," Art said tenderly, "you don't want him to say anything to hurt me. I think it probably hurts you more now to talk about my being unable to walk than it does me. But if it's about a paralyzed man, I think I'm the expert, don't you?"

nine

The wheels on the chair made no noise as Art swung down the path to the backyard. He saw no sign of the children but he instinctively knew where they would be.

As he neared the now completed kennel, which Jacky still claimed at times for a cubby house, he heard her shrill voice saying earnestly, "But don't you remember what Uncle Jim said? Jesus can do anything He wants to. If He wants Dad to walk again He'll make him better."

Art froze.

Jacky continued relentlessly. "But, Uncle Jim said we're not to expect God to be like Santa Claus. After all, there must have been lots of cripples like Daddy around that were never made better by Jesus."

Art heard a sudden scuffle. There was a cry from Jacky and then Robbie's furious voice. "Don't you dare call him that. My daddy's not a cripple. He's not. . .he's not. . ."

Jacky burst out of the rough shelter. "He can't walk! He is so too a cripple!" she yelled back over her shoulder, and then froze as she saw her father.

For one horrified moment they stared at each other. She gave a despairing sob and scuttled past him. Before he could do more than open his mouth she was flying toward the house.

He hesitated for a moment, not sure whether to call her back, but the noisy sobs coming from the kennel decided him. He heard Bonnie give a short, soft yelp and knew the dog must be as bewildered as he was.

Beth and Jim had both assured him that the children had

apparently accepted what had happened to their father. But now this small replica of himself obviously didn't want a cripple for a father. And who could blame him?

Art remembered only too vividly how he had always hated his own father being so different from his friends' fathers. Too many times his father had ranted and raved at boys he had brought home. Too many times he had shouted at them that they were miserable sinners when they had let a couple of swear words slip out. He would shout Bible verses at them, roaring out that sinners died, that they belonged to the devil and would join him in the fires of hell.

The kids had called his father a weirdo, a religious freak. They had teased Art unmercifully at school, and the older he became the more he had done everything he could to prove to them how irreligious he was himself, that he was nothing like his strange father.

To try and feel accepted, he started swearing more than any of them. As the years progressed he had become more and more rebellious, getting into more and more trouble for fighting, for smoking and drinking.

Then the police had questioned him about some graffiti and vandalism. Fortunately they had never been able to prove anything enough to bring charges. But his parents had not believed his protests of innocence. They had been so shocked that a son of theirs could be in trouble with the police that they had disowned him, kicked him out.

The irony had been that this time he had been completely innocent. But he had been relieved to escape from his parents.

Art took a deep breath. Suddenly he knew what he had to do. He whistled. "Bonnie," he called, "where are you? Come here, girl."

He whistled again, and then the dog bounded out of the shelter and pranced up to him. With relief, Art heard the noisy crying stop.

He patted the dog vigorously and said loudly, "Now, girl, where's that son of mine? I was very interested to hear there was a story at Sunday school about a guy like me who couldn't walk. Do you think he'd tell me about him?"

Bonnie jumped up, putting her paws on his knees. She swiped her wet tongue across his cheek. He tried to dodge her, but she gave a short, sharp bark and gave him another enthusiastic lick on his face.

"Down, ya big slobberer!" Art gave a loud laugh and yelled, "Hey, Robbie, are you there? Come and rescue me!"

To Art's relief, Robbie slowly appeared. Without any more prompting, Bonnie deserted Art and ran back to Robbie. Then she stopped. Her ears pricked up as a kookaburra chortled nearby, and she suddenly raced away, barking furiously.

Art shook his head. "She's one crazy animal." He grinned at Robbie, carefully pretending not to notice the tearful dirt-stained face. "Mum likes me to keep out of her hair while she gets lunch, so I thought we'd have a few minutes for you to tell me that story you heard today."

Robbie eyed him with a scowl. Then he looked down and kicked his toes against the edge of the cement path.

Art tried again. "Ah, come on mate. I really would like to know what happened to that bloke like me."

Robbie looked up at him with suspicious eyes.

"You see Robbie," Art continued seriously, "I think it might be the story I remember. . ." He took a deep breath and said quickly, ". . .I remember about a cripple. My father told me about it. Only, I haven't ever read it myself, and I'm not sure if I remember properly what happened. Was the man really paralyzed like me?"

Robbie gave one big nod. He took a step closer. "He. . . he'd been paralyzed and couldn't walk for a long, long time and his friends heard about Jesus making. . ." He gulped, and continued sadly, "Jesus made lots of people walk again."

A lump lodged in Art's throat at the tears that again whelmed up and spilled over in Robbie's eyes. "Look, Robbie, why don't you climb up here on my knees, let me park this contraption in the shade, and you can tell me all about it."

Robbie looked doubtfully from his father to the chair and back to his face. "Wouldn't that hurt your legs?"

"Well it didn't when your Mum sat on them," Art couldn't resist saying dryly.

Memory flared deep inside him. That day seemed so long ago now. He and Beth had been so close for such a brief time. He winced inwardly. It had been his fault that their intimacy had not continued. He had withdrawn again, and he knew that had hurt and bewildered Beth. But she had not said another word about it as he'd been sure she would.

"Would. . .wouldn't you like me to push you, Daddy?"

"No thanks, mate. I'm very handy pushing on these wheels now." Art held out his hands. To his utter relief, Robbie came forward and let Art pull him onto his lap. "Hang on tight now."

Art did one of his best wheelie spins and Robbie let out a squeal and grabbed him tighter. Art chuckled, and did it again. Then he had to do it again to head in the right direction. With satisfaction, he noted that Robbie was grinning from ear to ear when they stopped under the poinciana tree.

"I like this spot." Art pulled Robbie into a more comfortable position and hugged him close. "Right, now let's hear this story. I remember something about a paralyzed man whose friends took him to Jesus to see if He would make him walk again. Was that the story?"

Robbie nodded vigorously. "There were lots and lots of

people trying to see Jesus, and they couldn't get into the house. So his friends had this great idea about going up on the roof and chopping a hole in it and letting the man down next to Jesus. And they did, and Jesus loved him so much He told him to pick up his bed and walk, and he did."

Robbie paused, and Art waited patiently.

"Well, they thought it was a great idea, but I bet the man who owned the place didn't!" There was disgust in the small voice, and Art controlled his twitching lips with some difficulty.

"Oh, I don't know. The most famous person around was in his house. He was probably enjoying all the fuss," he couldn't resist saying.

Robbie looked up at him doubtfully. "How would you like all that mess in our lounge room?"

Art chuckled, and Robbie grinned back at him.

"Your mum would sure have something to say!" Then, all desire to laugh left Art. "If it meant a man like me could walk again, she wouldn't mind."

"Oh, Daddy, I hate it that you can't walk!"

"It's not exactly fun for me either, mate!"

Robbie sat bolt upright and Art tensed. The words simply flew out of the small boy. "Out at the farm I hated it that you couldn't go down to the sheds again and drive the truck again. And then at the wedding you had to go home and missed all the fun, and I asked and asked Jesus to make you walk again. And at school the kids called you a cripple and I got into trouble for punchin' one on the nose."

Art made a small sound, and alarm flashed across Robbie's face.

"Please don't tell, Mum," he pleaded. "Me an' Jacky decided Mum had enough to worry about without knowing that."

"Mothers have a funny habit of knowing when something

like that happens," said Art solemnly, "and sometimes they worry when they think their kids are not telling them things. So, I won't tell her this time, as long as you promise to tell her when you're really upset about something. Okay?"

Robbie studied his father's face. Then he sighed gloomily. "Yeah, I s'pose. And sometimes I hate this big school, and I hate living in a city. I loved being at the farm with Uncle Jim and Grandma and. . .But could I tell you first, Dad? If I get upset again?"

Art's arms tightened, and then he relaxed again. "Yes, of course, Robbie," he said quickly, "but I don't want you to ever wait too long to tell your mother if I'm. . .if I'm not here when you get home from school."

Robbie nodded slowly again.

They were both silent for a moment, and then Art reminded him gently, "You haven't finished telling me why you were so upset today."

Robbie fidgeted with his hands. "When the teacher finished telling the story, I asked her if it was a true one an' really in the Bible," he started slowly. Then he continued very rapidly, the words bursting out of him, "It can't be true, can it Dad? I. . .I told her I didn't believe Jesus did that at all because He didn't make you better at the farm when I asked and asked. . .an'. . .an' a boy laughed. . .and. . ." The rapid words and sad voice died away into a sob.

Art closed his eyes. His arms tightened around the small body nestled so trustingly against him. He had been afraid it had been something like this. All except that bit about. . . .

His eyes flew open. "Robbie! When did you ask Jesus to make me walk again?"

❧

Beth turned away from the kitchen window with a sigh. What on earth was going on under that poinciana tree?

When Jacky had raced past her with tears streaming down

her face Beth had nearly gone to help Art then. But she knew Art wanted to be the one to try and sort it out. Then she had seen him successfully coax Robbie out of the rough shelter, so she had decided to leave him to it while she dealt with their daughter instead.

A woebegone Jacky had cried, "Now Daddy will hate me. I called him a. . .a cripple. And he heard!"

Beth had managed to reassure Jacky that her father might be hurt by hearing that, but he would never hate his daughter. When she had returned to her vigil at the window overlooking the backyard, she had been filled with trepidation. Art might never hate his daughter, but she knew how sensitive he was about his disabilities. Then she saw Art had Robbie on his knee and that they seemed engrossed in whatever they were talking about. She breathed a sigh of relief and started preparing a meal.

As her hands flew, preparing a simple salad for lunch, she thought of the church service. Art had actually seemed to enjoy it! Her spirits lifted with hope. It was a start.

She was hesitating about calling them all to lunch when Art wheeled himself into the kitchen. He looked pale and strained. The expression on his face made her go cold.

"Beth. . ."

Robbie bounced in behind Art. "Mum, Dad said we can have half a day off school t'morra!"

He raced through the room, calling to his sister, all animosity forgotten. They heard him start telling Jacky they were to go to the hospital, then the bedroom door slammed behind him.

The small boy's face had been radiant. Beth's eyes went fearfully back to her husband. He had not moved and was watching her intently. His eyes still held a very intent, considering look, and some other element that for a brief moment she thought was fear.

"Beth," Art said slowly, "I want the three of you to come to the hospital tomorrow afternoon and see some of the. . . er. . .exercises I've been doing at physio."

Instead of feeling the relief she should have, the expression in his face made her begin to tremble. "Why? What does it have to do with what upset Robbie?"

He did not move. Then he said harshly, "He hates thinking I'm a cripple. I need him, you, all of you to see how much mobility I now have."

Very, very carefully, Beth put down the plate in her suddenly nerveless fingers. Then she asked the question that had been troubling her for weeks, the one she had been too anxious, too plain scared of the answer, to ask. "Does this have anything to do with the fact that you were able to be discharged from the hospital without an indwelling catheter, without needing help anymore to go to the bathroom. . .to. . .to. . . ?" Her voice faded, and she clutched the side of the table, staring at Art.

"Beth! Don't look like that." Art started toward her, and then stopped abruptly when Robbie raced into the room.

"I'm starving, Mum. Isn't lunch ready yet?"

Beth turned away. Exercising every ounce of self-control she had been learning the past months, she managed to say without a quiver in her voice, "Call Jacky. We'll start as soon as you're all sitting down."

Jacky entered the room slowly and moved reluctantly toward her place at the table, avoiding her father's eyes.

"So, Jacky, are you glad you're going to miss half a day at school tomorrow?"

She looked at her father, and hesitated. "Can I really go, too, Daddy?"

"Well," said Art very seriously, "I really can't imagine this mob going anywhere as a family without the best, most beautiful daughter a bloke like me could ever have, do you?"

Then he smiled at her.

Art's smile was full of compassion and tenderness, and sudden love for him burned fiercely in Beth. He always had been a wonderful father.

Jacky gave him a relieved smile, which dimmed a little at his next words.

"However, young lady, because I want you to stay beautiful, I think you should watch what you say in the future, don't you? And the way you say it," he added sternly.

She dropped her head and nodded vigorously. "I'm sorry, Daddy," she whispered.

"Well, that's fine then. Now, whose turn is it to say grace?" Art looked across at Beth. "I think it should be me, don't you?"

Beth's eyes flew wide. She nodded quickly and bowed her head. This was the first time ever that he had voluntarily offered to pray!

There was a pause. Just as she started to look up at him to see if he had changed his mind, Art cleared his throat. His voice was husky but very sincere. "God, we thank You for our family and all Your blessings, especially. . .especially for Mum and this food, amen."

Beth looked up slowly at him. He held her gaze for a brief moment, and then lowered his eyes to his plate.

Robbie had a suppressed air of excitement throughout the short meal. He shared several expressive looks with his father, and Beth could see they shared a secret. Once again, fear clutched its icy hand around her heart.

That night, Beth hardly slept. She spent hours reading her Bible and praying. In the early morning hours she crept silently out to the kitchen for a drink. A crack of light gleamed under Art's bedroom door. She hesitated, but then continued to the kitchen. On her way back to bed a little later, she was relieved to see he had turned his light off.

During the rest of the day he had had plenty of opportunities to tell her what he had meant about "increased mobility," but he had not taken them. In fact he had very obviously managed to avoid being alone with her. He had even refused any help getting ready for bed. Apprehension and that deep-seated fear that she had striven to overcome for weeks had stopped her asking any more questions.

By morning, she was very weary. The spiritual battle had been long and hard before she had at last been able to pray, "I'm so sorry I haven't been trusting You enough. I've been so afraid. Please take that fear away. And. . .and God, I placed Art in your hands long before the accident. Now I again commit him to You. I want what is best for him so that he might come to know You personally and accept that You love him. But, oh loving heavenly Father, I do need him to love me too, to believe that I really do love him."

She was silent for a long moment, and then she gave a low sob of submission. "But I yield our whole relationship and future to Your will for both our lives. Just give me Your strength each day, no matter what!"

In the morning, she and Art hardly spoke to each other before she left the house. He too looked as though he had not slept much, but she had refrained from asking. He had taken one long, hard look at her own face, and turned away without a word.

She had no problem getting a couple of extra hours off work, and Beth picked up two excited children at the arranged time. When they arrived at the physiotherapy department and she saw him, she knew her fears had been justified.

Art would very soon no longer need her, no longer have a reason not to move out again.

He could walk.

ten

At first, only Beth saw the tall figure leaning on his walking frame. "I'd forgotten just how tall he is," she thought numbly. "He's even taller than Jim."

Their eyes met across the room. He moved, slowly rolling the walking frame forward on its wheels. Without losing eye contact, he lifted one leg, stiffly, awkwardly, moved it forward. Then he lifted his other leg, took another small step. Then he straightened and stood still.

Across the room their eyes met and clung.

Beth began to tremble. She forced her eyes to break contact and looked down at the children. Then, helplessly, her gaze flew back to Art.

He watched her for a moment longer. He was very pale. Then his eyes drifted to the two children, one each side of her. Even from that distance, she could see how his strong features softened.

The frame moved again, followed by the slow awkward movement of two legs learning to walk again. The movement caught the children's attention.

"Wow, Dad!" Jacky exclaimed out loud.

Robbie looked up at his mother, his eyes dancing. "Did ya see, Mum? Did ya'?" He let go of her hand and raced toward Art. "Dad!" he yelled, and several heads swung towards him. "You *are* walking like ya' said. Jesus *is* making ya' better!"

A faint tinge of color touched Art's cheeks, but he merely grinned at Robbie. Then his eyes collided with Beth's again

123

and all amusement was gone.

As usual, not to be left behind, Jacky bounded across the room. Beth followed slowly, almost reluctantly.

For weeks now, she had been suspicious. All she had read about paraplegics in the early days in Sydney had made her wonder and wonder many times since Jim and Gail's wedding. And one part of her had been wonderfully glad for Art. The other part, the utterly selfish part she was bitterly ashamed of, had been tinged with a sadness and fear that had stifled the questions she should have asked.

She forced a smile for the sake of the children. Her chin went up. Her eyes challenged him with the question, *Why didn't you tell me?* But the words remained unspoken because she was so afraid she knew the answer.

"Well, aren't you the clever man?" She knew her voice had a touch of shrillness, and she took a deep breath. "I'm very, very glad, Art," she said steadily, and finally knew she was.

Art saw the hurt she failed to hide, and he knew that he should have told her. He had hurt her too much in the past as it was.

"I wanted to surprise you," he muttered, not quite truthfully. They both knew the other reason, but he hoped she heard the apology in his voice.

Beth's smile did not reach her eyes. "Well, you've certainly done that."

"Tell her, Dad!"

Art looked down at Robbie's eager little face. Then he glanced around at the other patients nearby and the couple of physios working with them. A few curious glances were coming their way. He knew the staff had speculated about his insistence that nothing be said to his wife.

He looked back at Beth. "I think we should wait until

we're home first, Robbie."

Robbie's face dropped, then it brightened. "Go on, Dad, show us how far you can walk."

Art grinned down at him again. "I'll have you know I've been walking for ages already today on this contraption, and if I'm not mistaken, my chief torturer is about to make me do some more."

He nodded toward a tall woman bearing down on them with a determined gleam in her eye.

"Right, Arthur, this your family?" The woman gave him no chance to do more than nod before she said sharply, "No more delay this time. Over to the parallel bars." She bustled away.

Art hesitated. "This is the hardest bit of all." He looked pleadingly at Beth. "I'm not sure if the children should see this. I only started this new trick a couple of days ago."

She looked from him to the two shining faces. "I don't think they will be content to wait outside now." Her voice was very soft. A gleam of sympathy flashed into her eyes and she added slowly, "You're not likely to fall are you?"

"I certainly don't plan to. But it wouldn't be the first time, or the last."

He saw her frown, but he merely pulled a face and started moving slowly to the other side of the therapy room.

They shouldn't have worried. With a few terse instructions, chairs were produced for the two children. They were sternly admonished not to make a sound, and then the "chief torturer" turned her back on them and started bossing Art around.

Beth watched with her heart in her mouth as Art discarded the walking frame and transferred his hands to the parallel bars. He stood erect, and then swung his legs forward one by one, while pushing down on the bars.

Then Beth knew why he had been exercising with hand dumbbells at home. He'd been building up the muscles in his arms and shoulders for this. Even on his first weekend leave after the wedding, he'd insisted on never missing his exercise regime until that last morning.

Now those muscles bunched with the effort. The physio watched him carefully, but Beth could see he had walked up and down between the bars many times before.

Then Beth saw a male assistant approach them with a pair of short crutches that only came to Art's elbows. She sucked in her breath. Then she let it out as a deep shudder swept through her. She couldn't bear to think of those weeks, those months of pain, the training he must have done even before being allowed onto the walker. No wonder he had so often returned home exhausted. And he had not told her any of it.

She saw the jaw muscles tense in Art's jaw. He directed one piercing glance at Beth and then listened to the instructions from the therapists. Obediently he slowly transferred his weight onto the crutches. He took a slow, unsteady step, and then another and another.

"Good. Excellent." The attendants were beaming.

Beth glanced at the children. They looked up at her with serious faces, and then back at their father as he walked toward them. Slowly, so agonizingly slowly, Art at last reached where Beth was standing, riveted to the spot.

Their eyes met and clung. His were triumphant, but begging for understanding, for. . .for forgiveness. Tears rolled unchecked down Beth's face.

For a moment Art was stunned. Beth was crying. Then she smiled radiantly at him. She brushed at her cheeks impatiently and he felt her lips press firmly on his. A fire leapt through him and he almost lost his grip on his crutches.

"You're walking, Art. You're actually walking!"

Art wanted desperately to reach out and wipe away her tears with the back of his fingers. Her skin always felt like soft satin to touch. But if he let go of his crutches to touch her he would fall in a heap at her feet.

Instead he whispered hoarsely, "Yes, Beth, they tell me not to expect ever to run again. I have to wear a spinal brace, but sometime in the future they think I may even be able to manage without crutches."

He saw the questions flash into her eyes, and he shook his head. "I'll tell you more about it when we get home."

The children chattered with excited voices all the way home, but Art sat silently, feeling absolutely drained. So, Beth knew now. Soon he would have no more excuses to impose on her generosity any longer.

His crutches were in the back of the car beside his wheelchair. He would still need the chair for some time when he had a long distance to travel or when he was too tired for the crutches. The staff had insisted he also take the walking frame, but he hated it and hoped he would not need to use it very much.

Each day now, his muscles were getting stronger. Each day he had less pain. Each day he was walking further.

He had no real reason to stay with Beth any longer. With community health care, he could look after himself. Though he knew she would never admit it, Beth would want him to leave again.

When he had walked out on her, he had been absolutely convinced she would be better off without a man like him. Nothing had changed. He was still his father's son. She and the children would still be better off without him in the long run. While he had needed her help in basic ways, he had been able to convince himself he could stay. But now. . .

Neither Beth nor Art spoke directly to each other until they were safely inside and the children had run out to Bonnie to play. Beth busied herself making a cup of tea.

Art watched her swift movements and then said, "Beth, did you know that Robbie had asked. . ." He paused, and then said stiffly, "Did you know Robbie asked Jesus to make me walk again?"

"Yes, of course," Beth said quietly, her face turned away as she searched for a new packet of biscuits. "We've all been praying God would heal you."

Art was silent. He should have known of course. For these Bible-believing Stevenses, praying for him would have been second nature.

He had been confused ever since talking to his son. Could he dare believe that God cared enough about him to answer their prayers, when he'd never even prayed for himself? He shook his head bitterly. Certainly the revengeful, fearful God he'd been brought up to believe in would never do such a thing as heal a sinner like him.

But what if He had? That thought had haunted Art every moment since talking to Robbie.

Beth poured the boiling water into the teapot and carried it across to the table. Still without looking at him, she placed a plate of chocolate biscuits on the table.

Art cleared his throat. "But did you know that the week-end we were at the farm *Robbie* made a very special, very earnest plea to Jesus to make me walk again because he hated having a father that was. . ." His voice cracked. He swallowed, clenching his hands on his lap, avoiding Beth's eyes. "Robbie hated having a father who was crippled."

"Oh, Art!"

He held up a hand. "That's not all." He was silent for a while. Then at last he shook his head, still trying to come to grips with it himself. "It was no doubt sheer coincidence, but. . ." He paused again, and looked directly at Beth. "Do you remember that Easter Sunday morning at the farm when I fell off the bed?"

Beth frowned, and then nodded.

"I had a lot of pain going home in the car." Beth's eyes widened in distress, and he continued rapidly, "That's one reason I didn't move around and stop that pressure area from getting a blister. It hurt too much."

Beth's eyes flashed, but he said quickly, "I know, I know. Serve me right for being so independent. But that's why I insisted on returning to the hospital that night. And at the hospital the nurses ripped into me too about being too independent. The doctor. . ."

Art took a deep breath, "The doctor couldn't at first believe that the paralysis in my legs allowed me to feel as much pain as I told him I had in them. Even. . .even that small tear in my skin was stinging by the time we reached home that day. I think the doc may have been wondering if I was just trying to trick him into giving me more drugs. He thought he had a drug addict on his hands."

"But you'd never take many painkillers because you didn't want to become one," Beth burst out.

"Fortunately, that's what the nursing staff managed to convince him. So, he ended up not only ordering the pain injections but a whole new set of tests as well."

The horrible memory of another reason why he had often refused painkillers made Art swallow. He'd never wanted to risk being tempted again to. . .Before he told her any more of this last incident, should he tell her after all this time about that other episode?

His hesitation was only brief. He had made the decision during the night not to keep anything from Beth ever again, no matter how it made her feel about him. She had a right to know what a miserable, weak coward she was married to before he told her anymore.

"Beth, did Gail ever talk to you about the first time she ever met me?"

Impatience filled Beth's face. "What does that matter now? What kind of tests did the doctor order?"

He ignored her last question. "Unfortunately it matters quite a lot. It explains why I've been so fanatical about tablets."

Beth's clear gaze became puzzled.

"You knew that the staff at the hospital in Sydney had been very worried about my increasing depression?" he asked quickly in an expressionless voice.

Beth nodded. "That's why Jean Drew wrote to Gail asking her to visit you. They thought you were still devastated about the death of her family in the accident, that it was preying on your mind."

Art hesitated again, and then he shrugged. In a clipped voice he said, "They were only partly right. They were right about the depression though. What nobody else knows, except Gail, is that I was so depressed that for a long time I'd only pretended to swallow tablets. I managed to hide enough sedatives and painkillers so I could take them all in one go and end it all. Gail arrived the very day I'd decided I had enough tablets to do it that night. She. . .she saved my life."

For a moment, Beth merely stared at him. He looked grimly back at her and he knew when she suddenly understood.

He had planned to overdose. To kill himself.

Her face went dead white. She stood up, then swayed so that he thought she was about to faint.

"Oh, Beth, I''m so sorry," he groaned, "I just couldn't see any future, any reason to live anymore. Maybe I even went a bit crazy there for a while. I loved you so much, and I couldn't bear what my being a paraplegic would mean to you. The way you refused to stop visiting me in the hospital made me know you would never agree to me living anywhere except with you and the kids. You didn't even go home to them when they were so sick with chicken pox. And I'd already ruined your life enough."

Beth sank back into her chair. Not once did she take her eyes off him. All along she had known there was something. Something to do with Gail. Something more than the fact that he had not admitted his part in pulling her from the wrecked car.

But not this. Never had she dreamed this.

A swift tide of fury surged through her. She felt its heat sweep into her face. "Art, you were so depressed you nearly committed suicide almost ten months ago, and you're just telling me about it now?"

For a moment her anger seemed to confuse him. Before he could speak she jumped up. Hurt and anger swamped her as it never had before, even in the darkest days of their marriage.

"How dare you, Arthur Canley-Smith!" she heard herself shouting at him. "How dare you not tell me something so important! How dare you make decisions for me like that!"

Her voice choked on a sob. Then the sheer amazement in his face spurred her on. "How dare you not tell me you could walk again! How dare you! How dare you not even tell me when you lost your job! How dare you think I'm such a weak wimp I couldn't be told the most important things of all! And how dare you think I believe for one moment that it was love for me that made you not want to live anymore! What kind of love is that? Don't you know your doing such a thing would have destroyed me too?"

Art's face paled. He seemed to shrink back in his wheelchair for a moment. Then he straightened as though recovering from a blow. The resignation and acceptance of her fury showed in his face.

Suddenly she was aware that the two children were standing in the doorway staring at her with frightened faces. Absolute horror swept through Beth. She had lost her temper. She was yelling at Art again, screaming at him as she had vowed to God she never would ever again.

Defeated, she sank back into her chair with a groan and covered her face with her shaking hands. "Oh, God," she groaned out loud, "I'm so sorry."

There was silence for endless moments. No one moved.

Then the loud peal of the front doorbell rang through the house.

Beth jumped. Slowly she raised her head and looked from Art to the children and back again. The children had crept to stand each side of Art. They were close to tears, and clutched at their father. He put an arm around each small body and drew them closer. Suddenly she felt excluded, outside their circle of love.

"I'm sorry. . .I'm sorry I lost my temper. I'm so sorry I yelled," she gasped between quivering lips.

Inwardly her heart was still crying out, "Oh, Lord, forgive me! I've failed You again. Help me!"

The urgent summons of the doorbell rang again. Like an old woman, Beth pushed herself to her feet and made her trembling way toward the front door. She rested her head against the door for a moment, desperately trying to pull herself together.

The verse of scripture she had memorized and repeated to herself over and over the past eighteen months flashed through her mind. The ninth verse of the first chapter of the first letter of John, the apostle of love. If she acknowledged her sin God was faithful and just and would forgive her, cleanse her.

Deep in her soul, Beth clung to the promise, silently pleading for His mercy once again, asking for added strength, for wisdom.

The bell peeled briefly again, and Beth straightened. Very quickly would she get rid of whoever was there. She knew Art had still more to tell her.

What tests had been done? Why could he now walk?

Above all, what did he intend to do now? Had she killed his love? Was he prepared to give their marriage another chance?

eleven

Beth stared blankly at the elderly woman who had given up and was already halfway down the ramp on her way out. "Can I help you?" she called in a husky voice.

The woman clutched at the rail. She turned and stared at Beth, before slowly making her way back. Beth frowned. She did not think she had ever seen this woman before, but there was something familiar about her.

As the woman came closer, Beth saw she was not as elderly as she had first thought. She was dressed all in black. Her clothes were clean and well pressed, but they had been carefully patched and mended in several places. Her hair was golden with only a smattering of grey, but pulled very tightly back and piled into a severe bun on the top of her head. It was her face, however, that concerned Beth the most. It was very pale and strained, deep lines edging each side of her thin-lipped mouth.

She looked at Beth with an arrogant glint in her faded blue eyes. "You took so long to answer the door, I thought nobody was home." The woman's voice was loud and censorious.

Beth was in no mood to be bothered by this strange woman who was probably only peddling goods or her own brand of religion. Before she could say she was not interested, the woman spoke again. "How are you, Mrs. Beth Canley-Smith?"

Beth frowned again. That mocking voice was also familiar. She knew this woman from somewhere. Then she remembered and stood frozen in shock and dismay. She had only met her once before, for a very brief time, at least eight years ago.

"Ah, so you do remember your mother-in-law at last, I see." Art's mother scowled when Beth continued to stare at her blankly. "Well, aren't you going to invite me in?"

Beth stiffened. "After the way you treated your son, and then me, why should I invite you into my home, Mrs. Smith?"

"Canley-Smith!" the woman spat at her. "Canley was my maiden name and don't you forget it!"

Beth's brain was clearing and she was thinking rapidly. She sent up another heartfelt prayer for wisdom. Art's parents had hurt him dreadfully. Since they had kicked him out when he was sixteen and disowned him, as far as she knew he had only seen them the once since.

"You didn't answer my question," Beth said after staring steadily at her for a long moment.

A faint tinge of color touched the woman's cheekbones. "Should I give you a reason for wanting to see my own son, especially as you neglected to tell me that the poor dear is now an invalid in a wheelchair?"

Beth heard the tell-tale squeak of rubber wheels on the tiled entrance behind her. She stood her ground and raised her voice. "Mrs. Canley-Smith, your son would never be a poor anything, no matter what his physical disability."

The tire sounds stopped. She heard a swiftly indrawn breath. She continued to stare coldly at Art's mother. "And yes, you must have a very good reason to come anywhere near us after all the years you've forgotten your son's existence. What do you want, Mrs. Smith? And where's your husband? Is he waiting in the car? Isn't he willing to be contaminated by such sinners as he once told us we were?"

Suddenly all the defiance went out of the older woman. Her shoulders sagged and her eyes dropped. "No," she muttered, "Art's father is not waiting for me." After a long pause she looked back up at Beth with a bleak look in her eyes. "He's gone," she said simply.

Beth stared at her. Did she mean he had deserted her? A movement beside her made her eyes meet Art's. Slowly she moved out of his way.

"Arthur? Oh, Arthur!" The woman started forward, and then stopped uncertainly.

Beth did not think she had ever seen such a forbidding expression on her husband's face.

He stared at the woman, realizing he had always felt rather sorry for her. She had also suffered at the hands of his father. Once he had blamed her as much as his father for the beatings, the hard work, the more subtle psychological punishments, the hours and hours of being forced to memorize scripture verses, the hypocrisy of their whole lifestyle. He understood now that she had been as much a victim of his father's religious fanaticism as himself.

"Hello, Mother," he said quietly, "what's happened to Father?"

A solitary tear slipped down the lined face. Art was startled. He never remembered seeing her cry before. He went rigid, knowing before she spoke what had brought her here.

"He's gone to be with the Lord, Arthur."

Art closed his eyes. He heard Beth give a soft exclamation. Her hand touched him on the shoulder. He reached up and clasped her hand tightly, drawing her closer, trying to banish the coldness that swept through him.

"I think we'd better go inside, Art," Beth said in a choked voice. "Please come inside, Mrs. Smi—Mrs. Canley-Smith."

Art hesitated briefly, and then spun around and led the way into the lounge room.

Beth saw her mother-in-law look around at the cheap,

second-hand furniture. Some had been supplied with the house, others she had carefully chosen after deciding not to move all their own things from the house in Dalby. Mrs. Canley-Smith very carefully sat herself down on the only comfortable lounge chair. Her eyes flew to the two, curious-eyed children staring at her.

"You must be Jacqueline and Robert." There was no softening in the harsh voice. "Hasn't your mother taught you it's rude to stare?"

Beth managed to bite back the hot words that flew to her lips. These were this woman's only grandchildren. She looked gratefully at Art as he moved forward between his mother and the children.

"It's all right, kids," he said gently. "What about leaving us to talk to. . .to this lady. I'm sure you've got plenty of things you could be doing."

He hesitated as the children retreated. Then he looked up at Beth pleadingly before turning to his mother. "Would you like a cup of tea or a cool drink?"

The woman relaxed slightly and to Beth's relief she said graciously, "No thank you, Arthur. I can't stay very long as I have a train to catch."

"When did Father die?"

Beth looked at Art. His voice was expressionless, but his body was tense.

His mother hesitated, and then said rapidly, "He died from cancer four weeks ago today."

Art didn't move, and anger swelled in Beth toward this woman and her husband who had denied the man she loved all the joy of belonging to a family.

"And you've only just got around to telling us?" she asked ferociously.

The woman looked disdainfully at Beth. "I tried ringing you at your house in Dalby. All they could tell me was that you were living here in Brisbane."

"And of course, you'd conveniently forgotten where my mother and brother lived," Beth condemned.

"It doesn't matter, Beth."

Beth subsided at Art's toneless voice. Then she glanced at him as he added quietly, "Why have you come now, Mother?"

An indignant light sprang into the pale eyes. "To tell you about the money, of course. Why on earth such a godly man as your father would do such a thing, I'll never understand! Such an ungrateful, wicked son as he had!"

They stared at her blankly, and then at each other.

"What money?" Art asked tersely at last, ignoring her contempt as he had learned to many years ago.

"Your father left you one-third of his estate."

Pity stirred in Beth. On her only visit to their property, the poverty that Art's parents lived in had been sadly obvious. Probably his mother needed his inheritance even to help with funeral and hospital expenses.

Art looked stunned. "My father remembered me in his will?"

His mother sniffed. "Your father knew what was fitting and proper. He left equal amounts of all his money to our church, his wife, and his only son. As soon as he found out that nothing more could be done for his cancer, he even sold the farm. Set things up real good for me so I wouldn't have to worry now, he did."

"He sold the farm?"

There was so much pain in Art's voice, Beth moved to stand beside him. She knew that the only thing he had ever regretted leaving was the small farming property that had been in his father's family for generations.

His mother nodded eagerly. "And a nice price he got for it, too. Sold just at the right time."

"So the farm's gone." Beth heard the sadness in Art's voice and face. "My great-grandfather pioneered that country."

Mrs. Canley-Smith pulled back her worn cardigan and glanced at her watch. "My goodness, I'm late. I'm going to have to waste money on a taxi," she said in a vexed voice. "Call me a taxi, Beth," she commanded imperiously as she started to climb to her feet.

Beth hardly noticed. Her eyes were riveted on the watch. In sharp contrast to the poverty-stricken appearance of the clothes surrounding it, the gold and diamonds sparkled and gleamed. Her gaze swung to Art. He too was staring at it.

His eyes narrowed, and then he scowled. "How much money is there?" he asked abruptly.

A look of disgust crossed his mother's face. "That is not a very genteel thing to ask me, Arthur." She fumbled in her worn old handbag and handed him an envelope. "This is a copy of your father's will and the address of his solicitor. He said he'd sort it out with you."

"How much?" he demanded.

His mother drew herself up. "Money! That's all you care about, isn't it? We lived very frugally as good Christians should. Your father made good investments. It's so sad that a third of it will now no doubt be sadly wasted."

"Mother, how much money did Father leave?"

Grudgingly she answered, "Your share comes exactly to five hundred and five."

Beth saw Art relax. In a gentler tone he said, "You'll need that for Dad's medical expenses, Mother."

She stared at him blankly. "Need it for. . .why on earth do I need your thousands when I have my own?"

Beth froze. Art just stared at his mother.

"Why are you looking at me like that?" she said sharply. Then she looked at her ostentatious, diamond-studded watch again. She groaned. "Beth, you haven't rung for that taxi!"

Art suddenly spun his chair around. He dialed, then barked a request for a taxi into the phone, before slamming it down again.

"It'll be here in a couple of minutes. You'd better wait outside," he said in a furious voice. Without looking at his mother again he pushed himself toward the doorway.

His mother frowned and then shrugged as though his behavior completely bewildered her. "I never could understand that boy," she muttered. "He was born rebellious and impossible to control."

"I'm glad about that," Beth was goaded into saying, "or he would have turned out as unloving and hard as his parents."

His mother looked shocked. "How dare you speak to me like that!"

Beth was trembling, worried about Art. "Good-bye, Mrs. Canley-Smith," she said and took the woman firmly by the arm.

The woman pulled her arm away. "Well! After all the trouble I've gone to finding Arthur for those solicitors, that's all the thanks I get?"

"Yes."

Beth was in no mood to be anything but honest. So this woman, who had only ever cared for her religion and her husband, had only come today after all because the solicitors had somehow persuaded her to. Probably threatened to charge her the earth if they had to do it.

The only thing Beth felt was immense relief when Art's mother gave her a look of outrage and stormed her way out of the house. Beth followed her and tensed as the woman paused at the bottom of the ramp.

"You have shown absolutely no reason for me to show you any consideration," the woman said self-righteously, "but as a good Christian I should tell you that I'm catching the train to Sydney where I'm flying to England to our church's headquarters. I intend to stay in their special guest house for an unlimited period, and I don't know when I'll return, if ever." Then the taxi pulled to a stop and without another word she rushed toward it.

Before it had moved away with its customer, Beth turned and hurried inside. Poor Art. How would he handle this last and hopefully final contact with his mother and father?

As she joined him, he lifted a dazed, pale face from the sheets of paper in his hands.

"It's true. Five hundred and five thousand dollars. My. . .my old man was a millionaire, and they always dressed and lived like paupers."

"I don't care if he was a billionaire, your parents were poverty-stricken in everything that really matters!"

He stared at her and then back to the papers. After a long moment he said in a voice that shook, "Beth, do you realize this means I can now provide for us very adequately? We can pay off the rest of the mortgage on our house. There are all kinds of ways we can use this to produce a regular income."

Hope died in Beth. Now he no longer needed her to look after him. He could set up his own home, employ someone to look after his needs.

"Has that nasty lady gone?"

Beth saw Art force a smile at the two wary faces peering around the doorway. "Yes, she's gone."

Pulling herself together as much as someone could who felt as though a bulldozer had rolled over her for several hours, Beth said tightly, "And gone for good, apparently. She told me she was on her way to Sydney to catch a plane to England. I don't think we'll see her again for a long, long time, if ever."

"To England! She hardly ever left the farm except to go

to church!"

"Oh, she's going to church all right," Beth said dryly, "in England."

Art stared at her blankly, then he looked back at the children.

"Are. . ." Jacky said in a small voice, "are you still mad at Daddy, Mum?"

Beth drew in a deep breath. "I'm very sorry I shouted at your father, but yes, I'm afraid I'm still angry with him."

"Mum! Are ya' mad at him for not telling us Jesus made him walk again?" There was horror in Robbie's voice.

"I hadn't finished telling her about all that, Robbie," Art intervened rapidly. "And your mother is angry because there are quite a lot of things I haven't told her that she had a right to know a long time ago. And I'm very sorry about that."

He was looking at Beth as he spoke. His head was up. He was still pale, but his chin was thrust out and a very determined gleam filled his eyes.

"Right," he said, "we're going to settle this once and for all. Out, kids." They didn't move, and his face softened as he looked swiftly at them. "It's going to be okay. Your mother and I apparently love each other enough to become friends again."

Silence filled the room for some time after the children had reluctantly disappeared.

"Do we, Art?" whispered Beth at last. "Do we really love each other enough? Can you really love me after all that's happened?"

twelve

Beth couldn't believe that he still loved her. And who could blame him if he didn't?

Art stared at Beth for a long moment. Then he looked down at the bunch of papers now screwed up in his tight fist. He started smoothing them out automatically, not really thinking about what he was doing. Then he tossed them carelessly onto the table beside him.

"Beth, what did you mean when you said that if I had killed myself I would have destroyed you as well?"

Anguish flashed across her face. The eyes darkened to deep pools of blue filled with pain and. . .and yes, love. Suddenly he realized how incredibly stupid he had been. As stupid as his parents. They'd read the same Bible the Stevenses had, but they had never really lived by its teachings. The Stevens family read the Bible, saw God as Jesus revealed Him, and loved. They loved him. Beth loved him.

Then Beth's chin went up, and she glared right back.

He had always admired Beth's courage. That day he had at last yielded to her pleas and taken her to meet his mother and father, he had admired the way she had faced up to that strange, savage man's fury. She had been so innocent and so shocked at how anyone who read their Bible and went to church could behave the way his parents had that day.

That reaction of hers had always stopped him from telling her the worst of the treatment he had received at their hands. He had doubted then that she would believe him. Now he had doubted how much she cared for him. He had sadly misjudged her. Beth had obviously matured, had grown up.

"I meant exactly what I said, Art," Beth said clearly. "I had never ceased praying for you since that first dreadful week after you disappeared. When you were in the hospital, God was still dealing with me, dealing with my guilt."

Art's lips tightened. "Your guilt? Do you mean your guilt for ever marrying an unbeliever? What on earth are you talking about?"

Beth wrapped her arms around herself and moved away. Her voice became husky. "I blame myself for the fact that you had that dreadful accident. If I had not made your life so intolerable at home, you would never have left the way you did. I could hardly bear the pain and suffering you were going through. If you had died when you said you were planning to, I'm not sure if my faith in God would have been strong enough then for me to have survived." A shudder shook her.

Art was appalled. "Beth, it wasn't your fault that I deserted you!"

She swung around. "Wasn't it?" she said sadly. "There was certainly no love or peace at home for you to want to stay. There wasn't even a clean house and kids that were disciplined properly. And your wife was nothing but a spoiled, nagging brat, who forgot to show you, let alone tell you, how much she loved you." Her lips trembled, and she choked back a sob. "I'm so sorry I killed your love for me, Art."

"Killed my love for— No!" Art stared at her in absolute amazement. "You really think I left because I stopped loving you?"

Beth looked at him from anguish-filled eyes.

"Beth, I left because I hit you! I loved you so much and

yet I still hit you!"

She stared back at him in surprise. Then she frowned. "But you never hit me, Art."

He stared at her. Speechless.

Her expression suddenly cleared, "Oh, you mean that last night when I fell and hit my face," she said dismissively. "You'd been drinking. You did give me a fright. It really jolted me into realizing how far we had both sunk. But I realized very quickly how much I had goaded you into losing your temper, especially when you were so worried about losing your job."

Art made a queer sound.

Swift comprehension leaped into Beth's face. "That's why you left? Because you thought you'd hit me?"

Art nodded grimly. "And because I thought I must be like my father after all, no matter how much I'd tried to convince myself otherwise."

"Your father?"

"When my father lost his temper he lashed out at me—physically—and at Mum too, although he stopped that when she threatened to report him to the leaders of their church—or sect, cult, whatever you like to call it. It's certainly not much like your church. But even the leaders drew the line at bashing their wives, although they believed very much if you spared the rod you spoiled the child, even if it meant a few broken bones here and there."

"Broken bones! Art! You never told me your father abused you to that extent!"

"Oh, believe me, Beth," Art said grimly, "I found out there are even worse things than bruised arms, legs, back, and broken ribs from being sent flying over a log. There's distorting the truth and being made to feel from birth that if you don't believe as you should, you're only trash, completely unlovable and of no use to anyone."

Beth stared at him in absolute horror. She had always known that Art had not been able to trust people easily, had always been inclined to downplay any of his own achievements. Never had she dreamed. . . . A groan burst from her lips.

Art didn't even glance at her. Now the words had started they spilled out of him in a torrent. "I had practically no contact with anyone outside our church who didn't believe what they taught. It was forbidden. I only started to realize how cowed and brainwashed the other kids and myself were when I went to a public school for the first time. The best thing my mother ever did for me was insist that she could not teach me at home past primary level, that I had a good brain and I had to go to high school in town. I've often wondered how she convinced my father, as well as the church leaders.

"Then I stayed with your family a couple of times. You were all pretty religious too. I could somehow accept sinners being different. I'd been warned about that. But your love for each other, and your lifestyle, really hit home to me that our way of living was far from being normal. So I rebelled in a big way. By that time I was getting big enough to threaten to hit my father back if he beat me again. Plenty of people, church leaders, teachers, dubbed me uncontrollable. After a couple of years Father and Mother kicked me out. Made quite a ceremony of disowning me."

Beth thought of the first time she had met the scared, defiant teenager. Her face filled with sadness. "That was about the time Jim became friendly with you, wasn't it? He wouldn't tell me much about the trouble you'd been in."

The angry, hazel eyes softened. His face became filled with tender memories. "Yeah. I'd never known anyone like him before. Never had a friend like him before. He's still the most loyal bloke I've ever met. He took me home with him. Your Mum and Dad. . ."

Art's voice choked and he stopped.

After a brief moment, Beth said shakily "Mum told me last year that Dad had told her once the only thing wrong with you was that you needed to be convinced you were lovable."

Art looked at her sadly. "He was a great bloke, your Dad. I was always so thankful Jim didn't mind sharing him with me, letting your parents almost adopt me. I think it probably saved me from serious problems with the police.

"I so envied Jim his family. And then. . .then he had a sister who was boarding in town going to high school. She was the sweetest, most beautiful girl I ever imagined existed. And she actually thought I was wonderful. Actually convinced me for a while that I was worth something. Actually loved me enough for me to dare risk marrying her."

His face became bleak again. "The only thing that worried me more than anything was that she was also very religious."

Beth gave a small exclamation, and he grinned wryly. "Oh, I knew from the start that Jim wasn't real happy about the idea of me as a brother-in-law, even through we were good mates. Remember, he tried to tell us to wait, that we were too young, had too different outlooks on life. But we couldn't wait, could we? After the first few years, though, I realized he was right."

Art swallowed. "Your being so religious and different didn't seem to matter quite so much until after we were married and started having children. But in the back of my mind, I've always known I was like my father, temperament wise. I was scared stiff that if I allowed myself to be sucked into religion again, I'd become even more like my father.

"Not long before Robbie was born I found myself becoming real interested and curious about the God you talked so much about. It scared me and I backed off. Okay, the God you worshipped did seem different from the hell-fire and brimstone type of revengeful God I'd been taught about, but I was absolutely terrified if I got involved even with your brand of religion, eventually I'd become as bigoted and narrow, even fanatical about it all as my father was."

He stopped and looked away from Beth's intent gaze. It was a while before he said wearily, "And after. . .after Robbie was born things between us just became worse."

Beth didn't move. The pain swept over her in waves.

He turned back to her at last. The anguish is his eyes was unbearable. A heartfelt prayer for the right words swept through Beth. She moved slowly closer and slipped down onto the chair near him. "After Robbie was born, I let being a mother and being involved at church get all out of balance with being a wife."

"And I was getting more work his first couple of years than I could handle. I was hardly home," Art said sadly. "We just drifted apart."

Beth looked down at her hands. "I. . .I thought you were accepting more hours because you didn't want to be with me and the kids as much," she faltered. "I also knew my faith wasn't what it used to be, and I. . ."

"And you blamed that on me."

Beth looked up. Art had a strange look on his face.

"No," she said sadly, "not entirely. We had been such good friends. We loved each other. We enjoyed doing things together. But all through our marriage, I found that what had been the most important thing in my life until I met you, my commitment to Christ, I couldn't share with you like I wanted to."

Beth hesitated, not sure if she was doing the right thing by putting it into words. "Please try and understand, Art. I. . .I don't want to offend you, or upset you. But no matter what a good friend and person you were, as a Christian, I was disobeying a Biblical principle when I married you. Jim has always loved you, but he was right to be worried. The scriptures make it very plain. The way the old translation of the Bible puts it is that I became 'yoked' together with someone who wasn't a Christian. It. . .it just doesn't work. Then I made it all so much worse by trying to nag you into becoming a Christian *after* we were married. Another Biblical principle blown!"

Art scowled, and she added swiftly, "I only realized after those counselling sessions with Rance Telford, that all through our marriage I'd been trying not to feel guilty because I'd been disobedient. So I blamed myself more than anything."

"I knew that, Beth."

Beth stared at him. "You. . .you knew. . .?"

Art snorted. "Of course I knew you felt guilty about marrying someone who said he didn't believe any of that. . .I think 'that garbage' was the word I used at times."

Brief, ironic amusement lit his eyes briefly. "Why do you think I went to church with you so much in the earlier years? But after I had a son who could become like his father and his grandfather, that was it. I just couldn't risk going anymore. Or that's what I told myself," he added after a slight pause.

"Art! You're nothing like your father!"

"Aren't I? I look like him. I have a temper like him. And Robbie looks just like I did at the same age." Then he stopped. A smile tilted his lips. "Except that I only realized yesterday that in one way Robbie's more like his mother. He actually believes in miracles!"

Speechless, Beth stared at him. Of course she believed that God was a God of miracles. The Creator God could do what He wanted whenever and however. She dismissed that thought matter-of-factly, but was astounded by the rest of his statement. Art was actually afraid of becoming like that hard, cruel man who had been his father.

"Art Canley-Smith, you're nothing like your father! If anything, you even look more like your mother! Not that I'm too sure after today that's much of a compliment!"

Art scowled at her. "Mother was far more rational than him. Besides, everyone used to tell me I was the dead image of my old man."

"That frown is exactly like your mother's was a little while ago!" she said triumphantly. "I bet the people who told you that were only toadying to your father."

Art became thoughtful. "Well, I do remember that it was the people at their church. It used to embarrass me when I was a kid. There were a couple of old ducks who always ooohed and aaahed over my curly blond hair."

"Your hair," Beth said solemnly, suddenly trying hard not to smile. "They told you it was just like your father's? Did you by any chance notice your mother's hair today?"

Dawning comprehension filled Art's face. "They were both blonds," he muttered.

All desire to laugh left Beth. She tugged at her own fair hair. "So are we, Art. Both of us. But I don't think that outward appearances matter very much. Neither do our basic natures."

She hesitated, but then she looked him straight in the eye and said firmly, "Christ can transform people into His own image when they trust Him as their Savior and obey Him as their Lord. I know He's still changing me all the time! I don't believe that anyone has an excuse because of inherited genes, or even their upbringing. Sure, the way we're brought up has a tremendous impact. It can leave us with difficult wounds to be healed. But we have to answer individually to God. Even if you and Robbie are like your father in nature, there's no way either of you need behave anything like your father if you belong to Jesus."

The back screen door slammed. Art was still staring at Beth, an arrested, intent look on his face as Robbie raced into the room. Then he looked sharply at the small boy.

"When's tea, Mum? Aren't ya finished talkin' yet, Dad?"

Beth's heart ached as she watched Art studying Robbie intently for a long moment.

"No, we aren't finished yet," Art said huskily at last, and then added in a much stronger voice, "now scat!"

Robbie looked with disgust from one parent to the other. Then he turned away, but they heard him mutter, "Oh, boy! You guys sure can talk!"

Beth suddenly knew that until now, Robbie had been wrong. They had not really talked like this before in the whole of their marriage. Too many times, all they had wanted to do was score points off each other.

Regret filled her. They had ended up being alienated, both so lonely. When they could have remained best friends, able to comfort and nurture each other, she had sought friendship at church, and he with his mates.

Reluctantly she stood up. "I'd better start tea, I suppose."

Art reached out and grabbed her hand. "Not yet, I still haven't told you about how come I'm walking. And that son of ours will be satisfied with nothing less than a full account."

Beth subsided. "Robbie prayed, and God answered a small boy's prayer in His own way," she said simply. "I just thought it must have been gradually happening."

Art stared at her, a look of disbelief on his face. Then he shook his head in wonder. "It's really that simple for you, isn't it?"

She smiled gently at him, and at last he looked away from her direct gaze.

"Well, I'm not sure whether it was God's direct intervention or not," he muttered at last. Then in a stronger voice he said, "However, my starting to walk did not happen gradually." He paused, and added thoughtfully, "That's the strange thing."

Art ran his free hand through the curly blond hair only slightly darker than his small replica's. "I've been trying to convince myself. . .It *has* to be a coincidence."

"A coincidence?"

"Robbie asked Jesus to make me walk again, and hey presto, the very next day I have feeling in my legs," he said abruptly.

Beth had been walking closer and closer with Jesus the past months. Immediately she knew this was no coincidence. She closed her eyes tightly, her whole being welling up in thanks and praise. When she opened her eyes again, she felt the dampness on her lashes.

Art studied Beth's reaction intently. He saw her lips move silently. Then she opened brilliant, moistened eyes and looked at him. Her face was radiant.

Art swallowed. It couldn't be! Beth and Robbie had to be wrong. The God he knew about was more likely to punish a sinner than do a miracle for one!

"Don't you ever dare doubt again that God loves you, Art," Beth whispered.

His lips were suddenly dry. He moistened them and said hoarsely, "The doctors said they can't be certain, but they think that the fall at the farm must have jolted something in my back that was pressing on the spinal cord."

A slight smile tilted Beth's lips.

He added rapidly, a little desperately, "You know that the scans always showed that there was a fractured disc. I was immobilized all those months while the burns were healing. The fracture did seem to have healed over, but they thought there must be permanent damage of the spinal cord when I still didn't have sensation. Now, they don't seem to know what to think, but whatever was pressing on the spinal cord has been easing off."

"It doesn't really matter the hows and whys," Beth said softly. Her smile was the most beautiful he'd ever seen. "You're walking again."

After a long moment, Art whispered back, "And I'm walking again."

Then Beth was in his arms, holding him tightly. He hugged her to him the way he had so badly wanted to at the hospital. He buried his face against her and inhaled the fragrance that was always Beth. Then he pushed her slightly away, and their lips sought and found each other.

It was sheer heaven.

After an eternity of bliss, Beth stirred. "Oh, Art, I love you so much," she whispered against his lips.

He groaned, and plundered her mouth again. When his voice would work again, he managed to say softly, "I sort of gathered that after your outburst just before Mother interrupted us."

She felt his lips shape into a smile against her own. Then he kissed her fiercely again before she could speak the trembling words that were bubbling up in her.

A long time later, he pulled back and gently stroked her flushed cheeks. "All these long months since the accident, I've longed to hear you tell me that, Beth my darling." She felt the deep sigh that shuddered through him before he muttered, "I was so scared I'd killed your love for me, and that it was merely your religious convictions that stopped you telling me you wanted a divorce."

Beth looked startled. "I was so scared I'd killed *your* love for me, and I can honestly say I never once thought of divorcing you. I. . .I was so scared that's what you'd want." A flash of sadness swept through her. "I have to be honest and tell you that I still do wish that we could share a common faith in Christ and love for Him and His church. But I married you because I loved you so desperately, and that hasn't changed. We'll work it out, Art."

She hesitated for a moment, then said distinctly, "This time, I won't nag you, Art. I dare not neglect my own worship and fellowship with other believers or my faith will suffer. If you would come to church with me and the kids occasionally, we'd be so pleased, but I don't want you to feel bad or guilty when you don't want to come," she added firmly.

Art saw the sadness in her eyes before she swiftly veiled them. Suddenly, he remembered his envy of Jim and Gail. Ever since the day they had walked into his hospital room and told him they were engaged, there had been something about them, an intimacy between them that he had longed for himself and Beth. Now a deep inner knowledge was telling him it was their common relationship with Christ that added that extra dimension of oneness.

"Beth," he blurted out, "I don't want us to fight about religion. But I do want us to talk about religious things. No," he corrected himself suddenly, "Gail has always refused to call it religion. I want us to talk about 'Christian' things. After seeing the change in Gail, and listening to her telling us about her conversion, I realized that I was really in the dark about what she was talking about. I want you to—"

The shrill demand of the phone next to them cut him off.

Beth had been staring at him, her eyes gradually widening as his rapid words shot out. Her face had lightened, and suddenly he saw excitement, something like hope fill her face.

Impatience ripped through him as the phone continued its demand for attention. Beth's shared feelings were reflected in her face as she stood up and reached for the phone and said a curt "Hello."

Her expression only changed slightly as she said unenthusiastically, "Oh, hi, Mum. What's up?" Then she raised an eyebrow and a look of surprise flashed into her face. "He is?"

Art hesitated, then he shrugged with resignation at Beth, forced a smile, and started his chair forward. Jacky and Robbie had been banished long enough. A feeling very like relief swept through him as he made his way toward the back door. Perhaps the interruption had been timely after all. If they had started talking then, it might have spoiled their reunion. So many times before, they had just ended up disagreeing violently about religion—no, Christianity, he reminded himself with a self-derogatory grimace.

thirteen

Beth hung up the phone with a slight frown on her face. She had heard a ring of excitement in her mother's voice, but Mum had refused to answer Beth's questions.

But, oh, why had she rung just then when Art had actually been saying he wanted to talk about Christ? No, she corrected herself with a tender smile, he'd wanted to talk about "Christianity." To her it was one and the same thing.

"Dad said that was Grandma on the phone, Mum," Jacky's disappointed voice said from behind her. "I did want to talk to her. What did she say about Dad walking?"

Beth looked over her head toward Art as he reentered the room. She frowned again, and said slowly, "She didn't give me a chance to tell her. She was real excited about something and wouldn't let me get a word in. Apparently Rance Telford's going to be preaching at our church here next Sunday. He's accepted an offer to be their new minister. She said some of them will be coming too, and she rang to tell me to be sure and go to church Sunday morning and support him. Then we can have lunch together afterward." Beth paused and added a little anxiously, "She sounded funny, like she was in a big rush. I hope everything's okay."

"Great," Art said cheerfully, "we haven't seen them for far too long. I've wondered what sort of sermon that guy could preach. And I'm glad you didn't tell your mother our news. What say we keep my walking a secret and surprise them next Sunday at church?"

The children chorused their excited agreement as Beth

and Art eyed each other. That burgeoning hope in Beth grew stronger. Art was obviously taking for granted he was going to church with them too.

"And *then* they'll all see for themselves how Jesus has made your legs work again, Dad!" Robbie's eyes were dancing, and then he frowned and sighed. "But I do wish we could all go and live back out on the farm with them," he said wistfully. "I'm sure Bonnie liked it more there too. It was real fun running over the paddocks with her."

Beth was still watching Art, and she saw a sudden speculative look cross his face. He looked thoughtfully at Robbie, and then at Jacky who was nodding her head in agreement.

"You really liked the farm, didn't you?" he said very thoughtfully. Suddenly he looked up at Beth. "And like me, you've always preferred the farm even to life in a small country town like Dalby, haven't you, Beth?"

Beth hesitated, and then nodded a little reluctantly. "I guess I'll always be a farm girl at heart." Suddenly excitement lit her eyes. "Art! Have you any idea how much longer you'll need physio, now? Is there a chance we'll be able to go home sooner than we thought?"

Art looked from her to his two children. "I believe it shouldn't be too much longer at all. Look, I want you all to realize that they've told me it's not at all likely my back will ever be one hundred percent again. That means I won't be able to go back to driving trucks or heavy machinery. And there are still months, perhaps even years, of hard work ahead to continue to improve my mobility."

Robbie's and Jacky's faces dropped, but Beth said swiftly, "Oh, I took that for granted. After all it's been months already since the wedding at Easter when you first started to improve this much."

They smiled a little ruefully at each other, acknowledging

that they both knew they had many difficult days still to navigate.

It was Art who said softly, "Day by day?"

Wordless, she beamed back at him as she nodded.

After a brief moment, he broke their eye contact, looked back at the children, and took a deep breath. "There's also something else. I've found that I rather enjoy messing about with computers. So I'm going to do lots of study about them, and see where that leads."

He looked away across the room to where a bundle of crunched up papers still lay. Then he turned back toward Beth. "It looks as though there's no need to worry about money anymore," he said significantly to her, "so why don't we wait and see what may happen. Perhaps one day we can live on a farm even. Somewhere not too far from Jim and Gail."

Beth realized with a slight shock that she had momentarily forgotten all about Art's inheritance. They had had far more important things to talk about than the money. Art grinned at her, and she smiled back.

"Your walking's certainly our most important news of all," she said. "Now, what about you tell us all about how it happened."

Art hesitated as if he wanted to talk more about the money, but then he shrugged and turned a little reluctantly as Robbie fired at him, "Just when did they first stand you up and let you try to walk, Dad?"

He made light of it all in front of the children, but in the days that followed, Art bit by bit shared it all with Beth. By the time Sunday morning arrived, Beth knew about the specialists who had examined him those first days after the wedding. They had not been able to understand his expressed wish that his wife not be told, but they had abided by his wishes.

"I was scared stiff, Beth," he had pleaded in answer to her glare. "It was like a dream, something that just couldn't be happening. I didn't dare get your hopes up as well."

"Protecting me still, huh?" she had said with a belligerent glint in her eyes.

"Yeah, I suppose so, but later on, I was scared you'd expect me to stop imposing on you, and. . ."

Beth had snorted ferociously.

Then he had grabbed her, kissed her senseless, but had the grace to apologize humbly. So she forgave him again.

The days when she had been asked to stay away from visiting him had been when he'd undergone vigorous testing and been kept sedated to keep the pain at bay.

During the rest of that week, Beth kept waiting for Art to mention something again about spiritual things. But he never did. Now that his secret was out, he gradually used the crutches more and more. Sometimes too much, Beth felt, but she managed to refrain from saying so, even when he was in pain from obviously trying to do too much too soon.

He was also very tired most days by the time she finished work, and she kept to her promise to herself to allow him to talk in his own good time. But the shadow of not being united in spiritual things never diminished. It saddened her, and she knew it always would, unless Art put his trust in Christ.

Another thing was troubling her. Each day she knew they were becoming closer and closer again. He took every opportunity he could to touch her. They kissed often. His kisses were so tender, so sweet and loving, but she began to ache for the day when they could be husband and wife again in every way. She was only too willing for Art to set the pace of restoring their relationship, but more and more each day she found herself seeking added strength and patience in prayer.

The week ended up being very tiring, both physically and emotionally. She'd had little time to speculate on her mother's phone call, but they all had an air of excitement in the car on the way to church. Jacky and Robbie couldn't wait to surprise everyone, and Beth and Art couldn't suppress their own delight at seeing the family again.

It's only been a week since the last time we were at church, Beth thought with surprise as she drove into the church carpark.

Art unconsciously echoed her thought out loud. "Hard to believe it's only been a week," he muttered, "so much has happened."

Beth smiled at him, but as she looked away her smile disappeared. If only. . . . She deliberately stopped that wistful thought, and instead silently gave a prayer of thanks that Art was at least going to be at worship with her again.

Because they had all been so excited, they were in plenty of time, and not a lot of people had yet arrived. Beth had tried hard to persuade Art to let her bring his wheelchair, but he had refused. He did allow her to let him off as close to the front steps as possible, and when she saw the couple of boys Robbie's age watching them alight with wide eyes, she suddenly understood.

Tenderness swamped her, as Art carefully made his way up the steps on his crutches, with Robbie proudly swaggering along beside him. He was a wonderful, loving, and understanding father. She was so grateful he could never be like his own strange father. But what an even more wonderful difference if Art. . . .

Once again she pulled up her thoughts, and smiled determinedly as she greeted the boys and the adults with them.

"Park the car, Beth. I'm fine," Art hissed at her a little breathlessly when they reached the top of the steps. "We'll find a seat inside. I don't think the folk from home have arrived yet."

Beth hurried to move the car out of the driveway as another car pulled in. She had just parked the car when Jim's Holden Commodore drew up beside her. Her mother and Will clambered from the backseats to descend on her, and then Gail and Jim were kissing and hugging her in turn.

"All of you!" Beth beamed at them. "How lovely."

"And not only us." Her mother smiled widely and gestured excitedly at another car pulling in beside them.

To Beth's astonishment, a radiant Hilda Garrett bounced from the front seat beside Rance Telford. Then Jean Drew was there also, and a strange boy who looked a little older than Jacky smiled at her shyly.

Beth looked at him, and her eyes widened as she glanced across at Rance and then back at the boy. They looked as much alike as Art and Robbie.

She looked back at Hilda, but before she could speak, Rance Telford said swiftly, "Nice to see you, Beth. I'm sorry, I'll have to go and find the folk waiting to organize me."

Then he bent and gave a blushing Hilda a quick kiss full on her lips and hurried away.

"Hilda! Was that. . . ? I mean. . ." Beth's amazed voice tapered off, as there were several chuckles.

"You'd better get used to them," groaned Jim. "They're worse than Gail and me!"

Hilda grinned at her. To Beth's delight she was the carefree, fun-loving friend she had known for so many years, and not the Hilda of recent years who had changed so much since her mother had died.

"Rance and I are engaged to be married," Hilda said with a proud glint in her eyes. She turned to the boy and smiled proudly, "And I'd like you to meet Rance's son, Nathan. Soon to be mine too," she added softly.

Beth shook his small hand politely and said, a little puzzled, "Hello, Nathan. I didn't know Rance had a son."

"Neither did he until last Easter," grinned the boy.

Beth looked at Hilda, who murmured quickly, "A story we'll tell you some other time."

"Well, aren't you a surprise! Congratulations, Hilda," Beth said sincerely to her old friend.

"Oh, there's more surprises than that," Nathan burst out excitedly.

"Nathan!" Jean Drew said with some asperity in her voice. "Didn't we say we'd leave that story until after church?"

"But you don't find out every day you've got an aunt you don't know about," Nathan said blithely.

"Nathan!" several voices chorused in varying tones of exasperation.

Then Hilda laughed a little shakily at Beth's utterly bewildered face. She glanced hurriedly at her watch, "Oh, dear, I'm so sorry, Beth. There's just no time to go into details now. But very simply, I've found out that Mum and Dad adopted me. My real mother was Aunt Jean's sister so she's my very own, real aunt. As for the rest, Rance and I love each other very much. We're getting married as soon as possible." With a mock scowl she added sternly, "So we can both try and keep this kid in order!"

Art turned a little impatiently to Beth as she slipped into the seat beside him only a couple of moments before the service started. He was about to ask her where on earth she'd been when he saw her shocked, dazed eyes.

"Beth, what's wrong?" he whispered in alarm.

She focused on him, and then reached out and grasped his hand. "Nothing's wrong," she murmured back in a trembling voice. "It seems we're not the only one with a surprise. That family of mine's just full of surprises!"

He saw her open her mouth to add something else, but there was a stir behind them, and then the family filed in. Jim and Gail grinned widely at him, Gail giving him a very cheeky wink as Jim hurried her past to an empty seat. Mrs. Stevens was suddenly there, bending to kiss him before she and Will slipped past them to sit beside an excited pair of children.

As Art turned back to Beth, his jaw dropped. "Isn't that Hilda Garrett and Jean Drew? Who's that boy with them?"

Beth gave a slightly hysterical giggle as she watched the trio find a seat close to the front. "Rance Telford's son, whom he only found he had at Easter. Hilda's engaged to Rance, and Jean Drew's her real aunt!"

She tried to stifle another laugh as Art gaped at her. "You're joking!"

Several heads turned, and Art realized he'd spoken out loud. He glared right back at one couple frowning at them, and then he saw Jim turn around and laugh at him. He gave Art the thumbs-up sign, and Art weakly grinned back in return.

"Beth!"

It was another loud exclamation. Their heads weren't the only ones that swung toward Mrs. Stevens. She was staring at the pair of elbow crutches propped against the wall next to Jacky. Excitement blazed from her face as she looked from them back to Art.

"Is it. . .are they. . . ?" her lips formed the words silently.

Art nodded slowly, and absolute delight and wonder filled

her face. Art was vaguely aware that the preservice music had stopped. A hush filled the church as he stared back at his mother-in-law. Then a great tide of love toward her filled him when her eyes filled with tears as she watched him stand up on his own feet to join in singing the first hymn.

The song leader couldn't have picked a more appropriate hymn, he thought, but although he suddenly wanted with all his heart to sing the words, his own voice was choked. "Now thank we all our God, with heart and sound and voices. . ."

The rest of the service was unexpectedly clear and sharp to Art. Some songs he did know and manage to sing, while others he hungrily devoured. The hunger in him that he had stifled so many times before welled up stronger than ever.

And then when at last a radiant Rance Telford spoke, everything seemed to gel, to make sense, and once again he wondered how he could have been so blind, so stupid for so long.

Rance spoke of God as a loving heavenly Father. Oh, he warned them that this Father chastised because He loved, but He only wanted His children to come to Him in full and utter surrender so that He might bless them with all the joy and peace that heaven could hold. He spoke of the Father loving so much He sent His only Son to show once and for all time what the Father was like.

This loving God desired to have fellowship with His people as a loving Father to His children. This God's amazing grace caused Him to pour out blessings that no one could ever deserve, so His children could come to Him without fear, with hope, with love, and obtain strength for each day.

Art felt Beth's hand slip into his. For a timeless moment his own fingers tightened on hers convulsively. He dared not glance at her.

"If you want to know what God is like," Rance urged the congregation, "look at Jesus. He said that whoever had seen Him had seen the Father God. Turn and look fully at Jesus.

"There's no doubt. . .in fact we all know only too well," he said wryly "that we're all sinners. But nobody's sin, no one's," he emphasized passionately, "is so great it cannot be forgiven. But until we surrender it to God, it separates us from our holy, heavenly Father.

"Christ has already paid the price for that sin," he cried out triumphantly. "God loves us! He longs for all sinners, all of us everywhere to repent, to turn to Him for forgiveness, to ask Christ to come and cleanse us, to give us a new life, a new beginning, a new hope, strength for each day, and a joy. . .such great joy!"

Rance's voice rang with conviction and a great joy of his own, and Art's pulses leapt in response. This man had experienced first hand what he was preaching. He knew what it was like to be a sinner. He knew what it was like to find forgiveness, a personal relationship with God.

This was what had transformed Gail. Art felt his whole being yearn for such new life, such joy.

And then Rance was asking, pleading passionately for anyone who had not come to Christ for cleansing, forgiveness, this new life, to make a commitment there where they sat, and then have the courage to move down to the front of the church and make it public.

Art froze.

There was a soft rustle of sound as people picked up their hymnbooks. He turned and looked at Beth.

As always, she was conscious of his every move. Without looking at him, she again reached out and took his trembling hand gently between her own. As she felt the tremor in his fingers, her eyes flew in alarm to his face. His face was dead white with strain.

Then she saw the sudden resolve in his face as the congregation stood around them. Still clinging to her hand he pushed himself to his feet, taking her with him. "Hand me my crutches," he croaked softly.

Anxiety filled her eyes, even as a light started burning in them. "Art darling, you don't have to walk down there. Just yield to Jesus right here. We can talk to Rance later. It doesn't matter."

"Oh, yes, it does, Beth. I just know I must."

She stared at him a moment longer. Then she felt her mother nudge her. Art's crutches were thrust into her hands. Silently, with hands that shook, she passed them one by one to him.

All around them, hushed, prayerful voices were singing. Beth could never remember afterward what the song was. All she could remember was the light, the determination, the moisture in Art's eyes as he turned toward her.

"Will you come with me, Beth?" he whispered softly.

All she could do was nod and follow him out into the aisle. She noticed Jim and Gail turn and stare as they moved past them. She heard Jim's loud baritone falter and then suddenly stop singing. Jean Drew saw them. Wonder and thankfulness lit up her face, and her voice rang out triumphantly.

And then together they were standing in front of a radiant, welcoming Rance, who clasped them both by the hand, before they turned toward each other. They smiled in perfect understanding with a sense of oneness as never before. They bowed their heads in prayer.

In praise. In submission and love to the One who had loved them all the way, and would be with them each day of the years still to come.

epilogue

Once again, the church set in the midst of grain and cotton farms of the Darling Downs was adorned and waiting for a wedding.

On this first day of the New Year, a light breeze had sprung up. Sweeping across the stubble strewn paddocks where the golden grain had been plundered, it brought welcome relief to the heat in the small, weatherboard building.

Art's gaze swept the restless congregation. They were all there. Marian Stevens and Jean Drew were in the very front row where the bride's parents usually sat. Both were gazing around critically at their efforts with the masses of red and white dahlias and roses that wafted their sweet perfume through the whole building.

Across the aisle from them, Nathan Telford was grinning triumphantly at his old friend and partner in mischief, the elf-like Jodie Morton. She was now sitting sedately beside him, having of course won her own way to have "Nafin" sit with her and her mother, Kim.

Jacky and Robbie were sitting beside Will, watching the other two children a little woefully, having been firmly forbidden by their distrusting grandmother to join them. They had been so excited all week at moving permanently back to the Darling Downs to live, although they were weary from the upheaval of moving house again.

Gail was sitting by herself in the front row across the aisle from Art and the bridegroom, waiting for Jim to sit beside her once he had escorted the bride down the aisle and given her away. She was gazing steadily into space, a small, tender smile tilting her lips.

Art scowled slightly. She was rather pale, and he hoped the heat was not too much for her in her condition. This morning he had caught her being sick in the laundry, and to his great delight she had shared their secret, threatening him with all kinds of things if he breathed a word until after the wedding.

Art glanced back at his mother-in-law and her friend. They had turned their attention to Gail. Jean was frowning. Suddenly Marian Stevens leaned over and whispered in Jean's ear. Jean sat bolt upright. "Really?" he heard her exclaim softly. Her friend nodded firmly and then both women beamed at each other.

Art shook with silent laughter. So much for Gail and Jim not wanting to distract any attention away from the bride and groom!

The bride was late. Rance Telford was exchanging nervous smiles with the waiting minister, his old friend, David Morton.

"Where on earth is she?" hissed Rance anxiously.

Art's grin was filled with pure mischief. "Probably decided she couldn't be a parson's wife after all!" he drawled. Then he relented. "Or more likely, probably still trying to find her way through all our stuff at the Garretts'!" He shrugged, "I did try and suggest we wait until after the wedding to move into Hilda's house, but I was howled down."

Trying to distract Rance, he added softly, "We're so thrilled Hilda's going to let us buy those few acres so we can build our own dream home this year." Rance's answering smile was vague, and with a soft laugh, Art gave up on him.

Never had Art dreamed he could be as happy as he'd been these last months. The crutches were still necessary, but the amazed doctors had told him that, at the rate he was improving, he would probably be able one day in the future to throw them away.

The bouts of pain in his back and legs, the endless discussions about moving into Hilda's old home and helping Jim and Hilda with the computerized business side of the two farms, even the occasional mild disagreements still with Beth, nothing had disturbed the deep, abiding joy and peace that was still transforming his life since his commitment to Christ.

The sound of racing motors came at last. A wave of excitement swept through the small church. Rance gave a sigh of relief and tugged at his tie nervously. Art grinned sympathetically. A few moments later David moved to his place and nodded to them both to take their positions. Confidently, Art leaned on Rance and took the couple of paces forward.

The music peeled out. The people stood. The matron of honor started down the aisle. Art devoured her with his eyes, not even glancing at the radiant Hilda following on Jim's arm.

Then Beth was beside him. Art caught his breath. She was even more beautiful than he had thought possible. Their eyes met and clung. As they linked arms, secret little smiles glowed deep in both eyes. Tomorrow they had an appointment to keep at Art's old football oval. He would walk its length.

But today was even more special. It might be officially Hilda and Rance's big day, but Beth and Art had agreed to privately, silently renew their own marriage vows.

God had given them a new love for each other. God had given them a new marriage. God had kept them each day, and He would continue to do so each day for the rest of their lives!

Now they were truly one flesh in Him.

A Letter To Our Readers

Dear Reader:

In order that we might better contribute to your reading enjoyment, we would appreciate your taking a few minutes to respond to the following questions. When completed, please return to the following:

Rebecca Germany, Managing Editor
Heartsong Presents
P.O. Box 719
Uhrichsville, Ohio 44683

1. Did you enjoy reading *Search for Today*?
   ❑ Very much. I would like to see more books
     by this author!
   ❑ Moderately
     I would have enjoyed it more if _____

     _____

2. Are you a member of **Heartsong Presents**? ❑Yes ❑No
   If no, where did you purchase this book? _____

   _____

3. What influenced your decision to purchase this
   book? (Check those that apply.)

❑ Cover	❑ Back cover copy
❑ Title	❑ Friends
❑ Publicity	❑ Other_____

4. How would you rate, on a scale from 1 (poor) to 5
   (superior), the cover design? _____

5. On a scale from 1 (poor) to 10 (superior), please rate the following elements.

___Heroine   ___Plot

___Hero   ___Inspirational theme

___Setting   ___Secondary characters

6. What settings would you like to see covered in **Heartsong Presents** books?_____

_____

_____

7. What are some inspirational themes you would like to see treated in future books?_____

_____

_____

8. Would you be interested in reading other **Heartsong Presents** titles? ❑ Yes   ❑ No

9. Please check your age range:
   ❑ Under 18   ❑ 18-24   ❑ 25-34
   ❑ 35-45   ❑ 46-55   ❑ Over 55

10. How many hours per week do you read? _____

Name _____

Occupation_____

Address_____

City_____ State_____ Zip _____

101 Ways to Say "I Love You"

How do you say I love you? By sending love notes via overnight delivery. . .by watching the sunrise together. . . by calling in "well" and spending the day together. . .by sharing a candlelight dinner on the beach. . .by praying for the man or woman God has chosen just for you.

When you've found *the one*, you can't do without *one hundred and one ways* to tell them exactly how you feel. Priced to be the perfect subsitute for a birthday card or love note, this book fits neatly into a regular envelope. Buy a bunch and start giving today!

Specially Priced!
Buy 10 for only $9.97!
or 5 for only $4.97!

48 pages, Paperbound, 3½" x 5½"

Heart♥ng

**CONTEMPORARY
ROMANCE IS CHEAPER
BY THE DOZEN!**

Any 12
*Heartsong
Presents* titles
for only
$26.95 **

Buy any assortment of twelve
Heartsong Presents titles and
save 25% off of the already
discounted price of $2.95 each!

**plus $1.00 shipping and handling per order and
sales tax where applicable.

HEARTSONG PRESENTS TITLES AVAILABLE NOW:

(If ordering from this page, please remember to include it with the order form.)

········· **Presents** ·········

Great Inspirational Romance at a Great Price!

Heartsong Presents books are inspirational romances in contemporary and historical settings, designed to give you an enjoyable, spirit-lifting reading experience. You can choose wonderfully written titles from some of today's best authors like Veda Boyd Jones, Yvonne Lehman, Tracie J. Peterson, Nancy N. Rue, and many others.

When ordering quantities less than twelve, above titles are $2.95 each.

Hearts♥ng Presents
Love Stories Are Rated G!

That's for godly, gratifying, and of course, great! If you love a thrilling love story, but don't appreciate the sordidness of some popular paperback romances, **Heartsong Presents** is for you. In fact, **Heartsong Presents** is the *only inspirational romance book club*, the only one featuring love stories where Christian faith is the primary ingredient in a marriage relationship.

Sign up today to receive your first set of four, never before published Christian romances. Send no money now; you will receive a bill with the first shipment. You may cancel at any time without obligation, and if you aren't completely satisfied with any selection, you may return the books for an immediate refund!

Imagine...four new romances every four weeks—two historical, two contemporary—with men and women like you who long to meet the one God has chosen as the love of their lives...all for the low price of $9.97 postpaid.

To join, simply complete the coupon below and mail to the address provided. **Heartsong Presents** romances are rated G for another reason: They'll arrive *Godspeed!*
